USA Today bestselling author Katherine Garbera is a two-time Maggie winner who has written more than 90 books. A Florida native who grew up to travel the globe, Katherine now makes her home in the Midlands of the UK with her husband, two children and a very spoiled miniature dachshund.

 www.facebook.com/KatherineGarberaAuthor
🐦 @katheringarbera
www.katherinegarbera.com

Also by Katherine Garbera

The Hot Cop Next Door
Summer in Manhattan

Christmas at the Candied Apple Café

Katherine Garbera

A division of HarperCollins*Publishers*
www.harpercollins.co.uk

Harper*Impulse* an imprint of
HarperCollins*Publishers*
The News Building
1 London Bridge Street
London SE1 9GF

www.harpercollins.co.uk

This paperback edition 2017

First published in Great Britain in ebook format by
HarperCollins*Publishers* 2017

A catalogue record for this book
is available from the British Library

ISBN: 9780008277857

Printed and bound in Great Britain

Christmas is such a special time of the year for my family. My parents were married on Christmas Eve and this year will celebrate their 50th anniversary. This book is dedicated to Charlotte and David Smith for showing me that the best things in life always start with love, laughter and family.

I'd also like to dedicate this book to my family and it's a large one, so please indulge me this list of those who I keep in my heart. Rob, Courtney, Lucas, Bobby, Josh, Tabby, Donna, Scott, Emily, Linda, James, Ryan, and Katie.

Chapter 1

Christmas was the most special time of the year. This year, Iona Summerlin had poured all of her energy into making the Candied Apple Café a Christmas wonderland. She'd started from the storefront windows all the way through the shop. Her theme had been the "magic of Christmas". Standing underneath the iron-worked apple that hung in front of the shop and watching as one of the crew on the lighting team she'd hired placed a large Santa hat on the apple, she couldn't help but smile.

The windows had been inspired by Frosty the Snowman and how the magician's hat had the power to bring him to life. Iona and her design team had come up with a group of kids in one window and a group of adults in the window on the other side of the door that were both looking at a very plain shopfront. Every thirty seconds a wind blew through the scene and stockinged caps, berets, and top hats settled onto the heads of the different characters while the backdrop changed to a magical wonderland of the Candied Apple Café with different chocolates and other offerings, including their famous Minty Cocoa.

Snow fell lightly on the sidewalk outside of the Candied Apple. *It's Beginning to Look a Lot Like Christmas* could be heard from

1

the shop each time the door opened and Iona stood next to her very best friends in the world. They were being photographed for an article about the hottest holiday places in Manhattan. And Iona knew she should be satisfied, but she was already thinking about next Christmas, and the things she wanted to implement for next year.

This holiday season they were competing with the big guys on Fifth Avenue with their window scenes, so she'd pulled out all the stops to make sure their customers got the maximum holiday experience.

And it felt like her work was paying off. Two different companies had contacted her about partnering with them for the New Year. One was a luxury resort chain, which even Iona admitted was a long shot. The chain had only twenty resorts worldwide and in each resort they offered their guests a one-of-a-kind experience and retail options that weren't available everywhere. So, signing with them would give the Candied Apple an opening into the luxury clientele market that Iona thought would be wonderful. She had a few concerns, though, given that Hayley Dunham, their head chef, was particular about who she allowed to make chocolates for their shop. So far, the chocolatiers she'd used were just herself and one apprentice.

The other option was a developer who was interested in helping them open a second location in Manhattan down in the old meat packing district, which had become a trendy food mecca.

"This is so perfect, Iona. I love the 'magic of Christmas' and I think you have really captured it," Cici Johnson said, coming up to her and looping her arm through Iona's. Cici was a few inches shorter than her. Her friend and business partner had an easy smile that matched her curly brown hair. She usually wore horn-rimmed glasses but had contacts in today as they were doing a photo shoot for *Manhattan* magazine.

They were all dressed like … well Mariah Carey in her *All I Want for Christmas* video because it was sexy, Christmassy, and she wanted the promo she'd arranged to be as enticing as it could be.

Hayley joined them, linking her arm to Cici's. Hayley had blonde hair that she'd had in a pixie cut but was starting to grow out. The three of them smiled at each other. Some days, it was almost more than any of them could believe. Of course, they'd had the dream of the café becoming a success but there were times when it was still hard to believe it was finally happening.

"Same. I just love it. This morning I stood out here with Lucy for a good ten minutes just watching the windows change."

"I'm glad. I already have some ideas for next year."

"Let's get through this Christmas season first," Hayley said.

Iona's watch pinged and she glanced down at the device, which was linked to her smart phone.

"Oh, crap."

"What?"

"I'm supposed to be changed and on my way to meet Mads Eriksson from the Loughman Group."

"If you miss it, then it wasn't meant to be," Hayley said. "And then I don't have to figure out how I'm going to train other chefs to make candy my way."

Iona had to smile at the way Hayley said it. It wasn't that her technique was different to other chocolate makers, it was that Hayley used her gut instinct to create unique flavors. She spent a lot of time coming up with them. Her objection to opening even one other location was quality control.

"Don't worry. The Loughman Group of hotels aren't going to scrimp on quality. It's one of the reasons why I'm even talking to them," Iona said. "I better reschedule this afternoon's appointment, though."

She stepped aside and made a quick call and cancelled the appointment for this afternoon. She knew her focus needed to be here at the Candied Apple Café. This was what had brought them to the attention of the luxury hotel chain.

Eriksson's assistant said she'd get back to Iona with a new time and Iona turned back to her friends. They were both so happy. Cici was a new mom with a cute newborn at home waiting for her, and Hayley was engaged to a man that Iona knew loved her friend very much.

"What are you doing?"

"Just thinking how blessed we are," Iona said, coming back over to them. "I want you to know, Hay, that I wouldn't agree to anything that would compromise our vision for the store."

Hayley hugged her close. "I know. But we have to think about the bottom line."

"We do, but we aren't in this for the money," Iona said.

"I don't like it when you say that," Cici said, adjusting the red velvet Santa hat on Iona's head. "I like it when we have a healthy profit. Makes my job much easier."

"Money is good. It's just not what drives us," Iona said.

"Exactly," Cici and Hayley said at the same time.

Then they all high fived each other.

"Do that again," the photographer said. "Girl power."

Girl power.

"More like woman power," Iona said.

"Woman power, then," the photographer said.

This shop had come out of the three of them dating the same guy and finding out about it. These women were her heart sisters and meant more to her than she could say.

***

Though it was only three days after Thanksgiving, Christmas was everywhere and Mads Eriksson, who wasn't Scrooge by any means but really could do with some productivity from his staff, didn't like it.

He kept his office neat and clean with only a small silver frame on his desk that held two pictures side by side. One of Gill from before she'd gotten sick and Sofia's current school picture. He looked down at his two ladies and wondered if he was making the right decisions for his daughter.

"Hong Kong on line one," his assistant said via the intercom.

"Thanks, Lexi."

He knew he had to take the call, but hesitated, reaching out to brush his finger over Gill's cheek and then turned away, reaching for the phone. *God, he missed her.* He tried not to. He knew that she was gone but there were times when he ached for her.

It had been a year but the pain hadn't lessened at all.

Death was permanent so why did it keep surprising him? No matter how many times he thought he'd made peace with Gill being gone there was always something unexpected.

Always.

Dammit.

He had business to conduct. He was good at his job and he didn't want to find himself in the same position as Amherst, having to justify his qualifications to the board of directors. He had to either motivate the Hong Kong General Manager or find a replacement; something he really didn't want to have to do this close to the holidays.

He had said he wasn't a Scrooge but firing someone in December really would make him feel like one and give him one more reason to hate this month.

He finished the call with a stern warning just as a text message notification popped up on the bottom of his computer monitor. His assistant, the usually efficient and seemingly unsentimental Lexi, had "elfed" herself and made that her photo on the company server, so each time he got a text, instead of seeing a professional image, he had one of her with a striped elf hat on.

LEXI: *Your three o'clock has cancelled. Can you squeeze in a meeting tomorrow morning?*

She sounded like her normal, efficient self but all he could see in the company chat window was that stupid elf photo.

Mads suspected Iona's cancelation of the meeting had more to do with cold feet than timing. He'd been cultivating the relationship with her since the end of August and she was very cautious about getting involved with another brand. He didn't blame her.

The Candied Apple Café was unique – a combination of handmade chocolates in the European style with locally sourced ingredients. Their chocolate chef was the daughter of famed frozen-food guru Arthur Dunham. Unlike Dunham Dinners, the truffles and chocolate treats she created for their shop were anything but run of the mill.

He heard the third partner Cici Johnson was a wiz at numbers and she had to be good to have managed to show a profit at that high rent location on Fifth Avenue as quickly as they had. Part of it was Iona's marketing strategy. She knew how to get attention and had used some events and advertising that was out of the box.

He was impressed with the three of them and wanted them to be part of the Loughman Group properties. But she had canceled. He glanced at his watch and then at his calendar.

He didn't have any more meetings this afternoon, which made him think of something that his dad used to always say to him and his brother when they were growing up. *The fish aren't going to jump in the boat unless you're on the lake.*

The lake he needed to be on was on Fifth Avenue.

He looked at the chat window and tried not to grimace. He knew he was borderline Scrooge this year, but still. It was …

Frustrating.

He wasn't in the mood for Christmas. Normally, he would be able to tolerate it. But not this year. It was the first without his wife and frankly he had lost the ability to pretend. To be fake happy and act like a jolly fat man might bring his daughter toys.

But nothing, no amount of prayer or belief, had been able to save his wife.

MADS: *No. I'll stop by the Candied Apple Café and see her. Has my daughter been dropped off yet?*

Lexi opened the door to his office and poked her head inside. No elf hat in real life. Instead she wore a cream-colored silk blouse and her short blonde hair was neatly styled around her face. No hat elf or otherwise was on her head. She gave him her usual cool, professional style and he had to admit, it was exactly what he needed. He'd scheduled as many meetings as he could for December. He needed to stay busy.

"Sofia and Jessie have just arrived at the hotel and they were planning to tour the gingerbread kitchen with Chef Gustav. Should I have her come up here instead?" Lexi asked.

Each year the New York Common created a gingerbread version of the Upper East Side neighborhood where it was situated. And this year was no exception. The display would be installed over the coming weekend and have a grand opening on December 1st.

Mads stood up and walked around the desk, smiling at his assistant. Jessie was his daughter's nanny. "No. I'll go and meet them. Thank you, Lexi."

"For what?"

"Putting up with my grumpiness."

"You weren't grumpy to me, Mads," she said gently.

"I was grumpy in my head at you," he said.

"Well, I think that's allowed. What did I do that bothered you?" she asked.

"Nothing. It was me. Text me if anything arises this afternoon. I'm going to try to get Iona to take a meeting with me at the Café."

"Of course. Have fun."

"It's the beginning of the biggest shopping season of the year and I've just committed to taking a six-year-old to a candy store;

fun's *not* the word I'd use."

Lexi laughed as Mads walked past her and out of the office.

He took the elevator down to the lobby and listened to the jazzy Christmas music. He exited just as *It's Beginning to Look a Lot Like Christmas* began to play. He hurried his steps, weaving neatly through the crowds; he'd sent his driver a text message to meet him out front. He saw the waiting car and made his way to it.

He had no idea what Iona Summerlin looked like, but he looked forward to meeting her. On the phone she sounded sophisticated, professional, and occasionally she was a little self-deprecating. In fact, he was looking forward to meeting someone who was as focused on business as he was.

Walking through the lobby of the New York Common, the luxury hotel refurbished from its 1920s glory to a fully fitted, five-star resort, Mads Eriksson couldn't help feeling a sense of pride. As CEO of the Loughman Hotel Group he'd been instrumental in buying the old resort from the family that owned it and restoring it to bring it up to the Loughman Group standards.

It was one of only fifteen properties owned by the group. Each was unique, with bespoke luxury indigenous to the country and city it was from. There were some features, like the high-end retail options, which were offered at all Loughman properties. Mads and the board had a strict policy of exclusivity with each of the vendors who were in their properties.

***

The Candied Apple was slammed with customers and everyone was working behind the counter. According to the buzz she heard around the shop and in the back in the café, the windows were a big success. Cici had left after the photo shoot to go back home to her baby, Holly. She was only two months old and Cici was trying to balance working with being a new mom.

Iona had jumped behind the counter, having grown up working in her family's department store so she'd cut her teeth working on the register and customer service. And they'd run out of the advent calendars filled with unique chocolate treats for each day. Iona had worked with a designer to make sure the boxes matched the windows on the storefront.

Iona wove her way through the crowd to the storeroom behind the kitchen where the boxed Advent chocolate calendars were stored. They had three more shelves of them and though they were already a few days into December, the boxes proved to be a top seller.

She jotted a note on the huge whiteboard that they used for inventory counts that Hayley might need to do more chocolates for the advent boxes.

Then she took a huge armful, trying to balance the chocolates while opening the door with one arm. Her mother was always scolding her for trying to carry too much in one trip, but it worked.

Ha.

She stumbled into someone, yelping as she lost her balance. The boxes started to slide as the man caught her and a child's hands tried to catch the boxes and keep them from falling.

She looked up into eyes the color of a winter sky. Grey and blue mixed together, she felt a jolt of awareness before she stepped back and righted the boxes she was still holding.

"Here's one," the little girl said. She had thick, dark- brown hair that curled around her face and her eyes were a deep chocolate brown.

"Thanks," Iona said, smiling a little ruefully at him. Her mom was right. Not for the first time either.

"You're welcome. Iona Summerlin?" he asked. His voice was rich and deep, brushing over her senses like the blast of warmth from a roaring fire.

9

"Yes … how did you know?"

"Mads Eriksson. We've spoken several times on the phone," he said. Of course, he was here.

"I wasn't expecting you," she said.

"My assistant said you were busy and she wasn't kidding. If there is a break in all this perhaps we could talk?" he suggested.

He was persistent. She liked that in a businessman. Her father, who was the one she judged everything else, including herself, by would be impressed. She'd looked at the website for the Loughman Group. Knew that Mads was the youngest CEO they'd ever had. He had taken the company from stagnating in a crowded market, to making it a unique and sought-after property group. She had noticed that his brother was also an operating director. No under-achievers in that family.

"I might be able to swing fifteen minutes," she said. "Why don't you two grab a table in the Café and I'll join you after I deliver these?"

She noted the self-satisfied look in his gaze. He'd gotten the meeting he wanted. But it was on her turf, so she'd be in a better position to stress the items they weren't willing to back down on.

"Sounds good to me," he said. "Come on, Sofia."

"Sofia, for helping me out, why don't you take one of these Advent calendars as a thank you?"

She looked up at her father and he nodded.

"Thank you," she said.

"Now you'll be able to count down until Santa arrives."

Sofia shook her head. "I don't believe in Santa."

Iona noticed the fleeting look on Mads' face but it was too quick for her to really analyze.

"That's fine. It's still a box of lots of chocolates."

"I like candy," Sofia said.

"Me too," Iona added. "Can I get you two something from the café? We have a rich seven-layer chocolate cake that is better than you can imagine. Hot chocolate, coffee, tea, cookies,

10

brownies are available too."

"Coffee for me," Mads said.

"Hot chocolate," Sofia said. "And cake, if I'm allowed, Papa?"

"Cake would be fine," Mads said.

"Great. I'll see you two in a few minutes."

Iona turned away from the father and daughter and concentrated on weaving her way through the crowded shop floor to the registers, to stock the advent calendars on the countertop behind the staff.

"I thought you'd deserted me," Nick said.

He was one of their new hires for the season. A college student who was hardworking and happy and that they would let take shifts around his courses.

"Never. There are too many people here to leave you all alone."

"Good. Once I know the products better, I might be able to handle it."

"Well, I'm going to get Hayley out front here to help you," Iona said, waving to Hayley to join them. "She knows the products better than anyone."

Nick turned to help another customer as Hayley arrived behind the counter.

"What's up?"

"Mads Eriksson is here. He wants to have a chat and I told him I don't have a lot of time, could you work back here while I do that?"

"He must really want us to be partners with his hotel chain," Hayley said.

"I think so too. It's good for us and seeing the shop so busy gives us a better place to start negotiating from," Iona added.

"It sure does. Okay, I've got this. Go and do your thing," Hayley said.

"I intend to. Also, Nick is newish so he might need your guidance on some of the products," Iona said.

"He's in good hands," Hayley replied. "Go work your magic."

She wished she did have magic, but everything she'd gotten had been from working hard and trying to prove to herself that she was just as good at business as her father was.

Chapter 2

Sofia watched Iona as she approached their table with a tray of hot drinks and snacks. He hoped it was only his imagination but he thought he saw a wistful longing in his daughter's eyes.

He got up and went to Iona. "I'll take that."

She gave him a smile and tipped her head, the bells on the end of her hat jingling as she did so. She handed him the tray. "Thank you. Hey, before we get back over there, what's the deal with Santa and Sofia?"

"She … her mom had been sick with cancer since Sofia was two and she died last Christmas. It just sort of turned into a thing in kindergarten where she thought if she asked Santa to cure Gill then she'd get better. Gill passed away two days after Christmas."

"Oh, Mads. I'm so sorry," she said, squeezing his shoulder. "I won't bring Santa up again."

He glanced over at Sofia, who was playing a game on his phone. She often logged onto his device whenever she wanted to play. "It's okay if you do. I think she's trying to figure out what's real and what's not."

"Fair enough," Iona said. "I know asking about that probably wasn't what you anticipated at the start of our meeting but I

13

wanted to be careful about what I said around her."

Mads nodded. "Fair enough. Does this mean you see me as a person now and not a corporate entity?"

"I already did. Part of the reason I took your call was to see what *you* could bring to the Candied Apple Café, not what the Loughman Group could," Iona said over her shoulder as she walked toward the table.

The fur-lined, red velvet skirt she wore swished back and forth around her legs and he noticed that the bells on her hat were still jingling. The customers in the café all smiled as she walked past and for the first time this December, he felt like smiling himself.

Sofia put the phone down as he arrived at the table and Iona took the smaller mug of hot chocolate topped with whipped cream and red and green colored sugar, placing it in front of Sofia, then added the slice of chocolate cake. She put a mug down in front of his spot and then took the last mug for herself.

Sofia held the cocoa loosely in her hands, one of her inky black curls falling over her eyes as she leaned forward to blow on the hot drink. Losing her mother had been a deep blow to her and Mads had wanted to protect his daughter from ever experiencing that kind of heartbreak again.

He'd had to make choices when Gill had died and one of them was no more pretending with his daughter. He'd had enough of doctors who made promises that couldn't be kept. Nurses who had told him things to make him feel better that weren't based on truth. But he'd never expected that reality to kill her joy of Christmas and he'd been struggling this holiday season, since she'd been very vocal about not believing any more.

But he'd worry about that later. He was here for business. The sooner he got this finished, maybe he'd be able to do something with Sofia that would help to get her into the holiday spirit.

"How's the cake, Sof?" he asked as she finished her first bite.

"Yummy," she said, turning her attention to it. He'd allowed her nanny Jessie to run into the Ralph Lauren Polo store a block or so away to pick up an order she'd placed and Mads knew she'd be back soon and then he'd be able to talk to Iona about the Loughman Group's proposition.

"Glad to hear it," he said, taking a sip of his coffee.

"Iona, darling, the shop looks fabulous," an older woman, probably in her sixties though she looked more like she was in her forties, came over to their table. She had the same reddish hair as Iona but it was shot through with strands of gray. Her hair was pulled back at the nape in a chignon and she had on a slim-fitting sheath that flattered her figure. She wore a strand of pearls and arrived on a wave of expensive-smelling perfume.

"Thank you, Mom," Iona said, standing up to hug her mother.

Mads stood up as well.

"Mom, this is Mads Eriksson of the Loughman Group and his daughter Sofia. Mads, this is Valentina Summerlin."

"Very nice to meet you," Mads said, holding out his hand.

Valentina placed hers in his fingertips first, which left him trying to awkwardly shake it. He let it drop as she turned to his daughter. "Aren't you cute as a button?"

Sofia just smiled up at her. "Thank you, ma'am."

"Mom, would you like to join us?"

"Just for a moment, darling," Valentina said.

Mads offered her his chair and then turned to find another one and went to retrieve it. When he returned, Valentina was talking to Sofia. Telling her about a breakfast with Santa on the coming Saturday.

"You and your father can come as my personal guests even though the event is sold out. I'm sure you want to get your wish list in early."

"I don't believe in Santa," Sofia said, putting her fork down.

Valentina looked over at him but before she could speak, Iona put her hand on her mother's wrist. "It's just a fun holiday breakfast, really. And she didn't mention that you get the chance

15

to help out some kids by bringing toys for the NYC Children's Foundation."

"That sounds like fun. What do you think, Papa?" Sofia asked him.

"We'll see," he said.

"I hope to see you there? Is it okay if I believe in Santa?" Valentina asked.

"You're entitled to believe in anything," Sofia said. "That's what Papa says."

"That's very wise."

She smiled over at him. "My Papa is the best dad in the world."

"Yes, he is," Valentina said. "Not all papas listen to their daughters."

Iona raised both eyebrows at her mother and she just pursed her lips. "I should be going. I hope to see you both on Saturday."

***

Iona walked her mom out of the Candied Apple Café. "Sorry about that darling. I just wanted to make sure that little girl knew how lucky she was to have a good father."

"Mom," she warned her mother. Her father had been very hard on Iona growing up. He'd expected her to be at least as good as Theo had been, and her younger brother was very good at most things he'd attempted. "Dad was doing the best he could."

"He was. But he could have been more … understanding at times. I know he feared that you'd be too much like me."

"Like you?" she asked. "Maybe he didn't think the world was ready for two Wonder Women."

"Probably he was afraid I'd turn you towards charitable foundations instead of a profit-generating company. You know he wanted you to take over Summerlin Industries."

"I know. But it wasn't for me," she said. She and her father had had a strained relationship. And though she'd tried to always pretend she understood, she never really had. She had worked hard and had craved some sort of praise from him that had never come.

Her parents' relationship had been strained because of her mother's desire to *give away all his money*, as his father liked to say. And her mom's desire to protect her children from his fierce temper. She'd been torn between wanting to be her own woman and rejecting her demanding father and that need for his approval. She knew that had been reflected in the men she'd dated.

"I'll see you on Saturday," Iona said.

"Darling, Theo is bringing Nico," her mom replied.

"Well, I'm happy for them."

"I am too. My sweet baby boy is happy," Valentina said. Her mom hadn't been overjoyed at first that Theo had fallen in love with Nico — the man the matchmaker had chosen for Iona — but that had more to do with seeing one's child unhappy than with Theo's preferences. Her mother had always wanted them to be true to themselves.

"Thanks for letting me know," Iona said as her mom left. Sofia and her nanny were walking out as she went back inside, and Sofia waved at her as they passed.

She stood there in the middle of the Candied Apple Café and just let the rush of people, the Christmas music, and the smell of chocolate soothe that part of her that was wounded. She had so much, so many blessings. She was so lucky.

Now she had to go see if she could talk Mads into giving into Hayley's kitchen demands. Something she suspected he wasn't going to go for. He struck her as a man who came to the bargaining table with a list of things that he wouldn't settle for. And having Hayley approve the kitchen staff at each location didn't seem like the kind of control that he'd concede to.

Mads was talking to Carolyn, the assistant manager of the retail operation, when Iona approached. He ended the conversation and turned toward her.

"I see you are getting the scoop from Carolyn?" Iona remarked.

"Nothing gossipy. I wanted to know what she thought made the Candied Apple so popular," Mads said.

"What did she say?"

Mads put his hand on her elbow and she felt a little tingle of awareness shoot up her arm as he drew her away from the counters, toward a quiet area of the store.

"She said she couldn't put her finger on it, but she said that you and your partners created an atmosphere that was welcoming to the customer and that you made coming to work fun."

Iona hadn't heard that before. "That's sweet. Carolyn is a godsend. She'd been working for a high-end retailer when we hired her and she had a lot of insights into how we should set up the retail section. I don't know what we would have done without her."

Mads nodded. "I think you'll find that is the same ethos that we have at the Loughman Group. We prize our people over the bottom line. Of course, we want to make a profit but we've found — as I'm sure you have — that staff who feel like they are a part of the business enjoy their jobs and work harder."

Iona had to smile at the way he said it and if she hadn't read that statement on their website, it might have had a bit more impact. But she also could tell from the tone of his voice that he was sincere. "I like that. In fact, it's one of the reasons why we are entertaining your proposition."

"Good," he said. "Why don't you show me around the store? I know you mentioned being on a tight schedule so a quick tour will be fine. I believe Lexi is working with you to set up another appointment."

She showed him around the store, careful to keep the focus on business, but she liked the easy charm he had and how he understood that the customer came first. In the ten minutes she'd allotted for them to talk, she had to stop several times to help a customer with a product and Mads just stood there watching.

18

She was afraid she might have given him some sort of insight into the business she hadn't meant to, but honestly, how could it hurt him to know how much the Candied Apple Café meant to herself and her partners?

"Sorry, I'm out of time, but I do look forward to talking to you again," Iona said at last.

"That's alright. When you come to the Common I'll show you around. I think it will help you to see what a good fit our two companies are."

She just smiled and waved as he said goodbye. She wasn't going to allude to anything yet. One lesson that she'd learned from her father that had stuck was to never show her cards to someone sitting across the negotiating table.

***

Saturday dawned blustery and cold. Perfect for getting in the mood for Christmas. Iona was having a tree delivered later that evening but this morning she had the "Brunch with Santa" her mom had organized for Catholic charities.

Iona checked her phone, hoping for an urgent message from Cici or Hayley that would have given her the perfect excuse to skip it but there was just a cheery photo of Cici's baby Holly sleeping in their group chat.

Iona was one of Holly's godmothers — Hayley being the other — and she admitted she was in love with the tiny baby. Cici having a baby had kind of awakened something unexpected in Iona. She'd never thought she wanted a family, preferring business and, given her track record with men, that was a good thing, but holding Holly had made her feel ... well, like maybe someday if the right guy came along, she'd consider having a family.

She texted back a bunch of emojis and then mentioned the Santa brunch thing in case Cici wanted to bring Holly. She'd be so cute and would provide a distraction from her brother and his new boyfriend. She still felt kind of like something was wrong with her that even a matchmaker couldn't find her a guy.

Which was fine.

Really.

She had enough to keep her busy at work. The Candied Apple Café made her happy. She hopped out of bed, showered, and dressed in a pair of red and white striped leggings and an over-sized cream-colored sweater. She braided her hair before putting on her knee-high black boots, grabbing the large Land's End tote full of dry goods to be donated at the breakfast and headed out the door.

She pushed the button for the elevator and heard someone coming behind her, and glancing over her shoulder, she was surprised to see that it was Mads and Sofia.

"Hiya," she said. "I guess we're neighbors."

"Hi back. We just moved in back in September," Mads said.

"I think you'll love the building," Iona said. She couldn't help but notice how the gray argyle sweater Mads wore brought out the stormy gray color in his eyes.

"Some of the kids in my class live here too," Sofia said. "Are you going to the breakfast thing with your mom?"

"I am," Iona said. "Are you guys?"

Sofia got a stubborn look on her face before turning her head down to look at her feet. "Yes."

She glanced at Mads and he shrugged. "We are trying to do new things this year and seeing Santa isn't a bad idea."

Sofia didn't say anything else and sort of pouted on the way down. Mads didn't seem too upset with his daughter. She had the feeling he just didn't know what to do.

"I have a car and driver if you want to ride with us," Mads asked.

"Thank you." Iona thought maybe the two of them could use a buffer so smiled and joined them in their car. It was heated and warm as she slipped inside and slid across the seat. Sofia got in next and put on her seatbelt and Mads closed the door, getting in the front in the passenger seat inside.

Iona realized she hadn't been with a child since she herself was one and had no idea what to talk to Sofia about. The little girl didn't seem bothered by the silence and stared out of the window as they drove through the city.

"What's your favorite part about winter?" Iona asked, already knowing that Christmas was a sensitive subject for Sofia.

The little girl shrugged.

"I used to love a good snow because that meant school would be closed," Iona said.

"I like snow too. Last year Papa and Uncle Piers took me skiing in Vermont. That was funny because Papa kept falling down."

"I didn't keep falling down, Sof," Mads said from the front seat. "It happened one time when Uncle Piers shoved me."

Sofia giggled.

And Iona had to smile at that. "Theo — that's my brother — used to always try to beat me to get outside when we were growing up so he could hit me with a snowball."

"Did he do it?" Sofia asked.

"Sometimes. He's got a really good throw so I sometimes I had to sneak out the back to get him."

"We had a snowball fight too," Sofia said. "I won. Papa and Uncle Piers were covered in snow."

Iona smiled as the little girl entertained her with more memories from their Vermont ski holiday. And she glanced up and saw that Mads was watching his daughter in the rearview mirror.

He caught her eye and mouthed the words *thank you*.

She nodded. They pulled up at the center where the event was being held and the driver got out to open the door for her.

She hopped out of the car and waited for them. There was a line to get in and they were separated. Iona dropped off her donated goods and caught a glimpse of her brother and Nico

21

handing out bags to each of the kids after they visited Santa.

She'd go over, say hi, and then find her mom and leave. She didn't want to be the awkward third wheel at this thing.

"Iona?"

She turned to find Mads standing a few feet away from her with his cell phone in one hand and Sofia next to him.

"Yes."

"Would you mind taking Sofia to the gingerbread decorating area? There is an emergency at the Common and I have to be on the phone so won't be able to help her," Mads said.

"Sure. It will be fun," Iona said, holding her hand out to Sofia, who took it readily.

She was aware of Mads getting on his phone as they walked away.

Chapter 3

The gingerbread cookie decorating area smelled wonderfully of her childhood home. Ginger and cloves were the spices her paternal grandmother used to make gingerbread from scratch every holiday season. Her Grandma had died when she'd turned twenty-five and Iona still missed her, but it seemed keener at the holidays. The attendant handed a Santa hat to Iona and put one on Sofia's head.

Iona flicked the end of the hat and Sofia smiled as the bell jingled.

"It's okay to wear it for the bells," Iona said. "But if you want to take it off that's okay too."

Sofia looked up at her. "I'd rather not wear it, but you can."

"I will," Iona said, handing Sofia's hat back to the attendant and putting hers on.

She led the way into the decorating area.

She and her brother had always been close and thicker than thieves at the holidays, eating the candy meant for the Victorian gingerbread house decoration while no one was looking.

Even though they were in the same room, she snapped pictures of piles of candy and texted it to Theo with the caption: *Eating all the decorations!*

23

She closed her eyes for a moment, remembering that happy time during her childhood.

She and Theo trying to figure out how to move forward with their relationship, given the fact that the man Theo had fallen in love with had been hand-picked for her first. But it was hard. Nico had been living a double life and she understood how hard it was to balance being true to himself and managing his family's expectations for him.

And she loved her brother. They had always been very close. This hurt more because she had hoped by doing this, by using the matchmaker, she might find the one person who she could call her own. And she hadn't.

She shook her head and the bell on her long Santa hat jingled, causing Sofia to smile. There was a little girl desperately deter-mined to please her father — something that Iona was all too familiar with — and who probably would like something to believe in.

Sofia, who stood next to Iona, stared at the piles of gumdrops, small chocolate buttons and long multi-colored candy vines. She knew Sofia was too well behaved to take one. So Iona glanced around to make sure no one was watching before she took a handful of the chocolate buttons and held them out to her.

"Want one?"

Sofia turned her head left and right, making sure no one could see them before she took a small part of the handful that Iona had taken. She popped them into her mouth and Iona did the same.

"Yum. These are good."

"They are. Do you think anyone would notice if I took a gumdrop?" Sofia asked.

"Which color?" Iona replied.

"Green," Sofia said.

Iona carefully picked out one green gumdrop and playfully handed it to Sofia, who popped it into her mouth. Then she took a white one for herself.

"I see we have two eager helpers waiting to decorate," one of the volunteers said as he came over.

He was young, in his early twenties, with a close-cropped haircut and an easy smile. As he stooped down to talk to Sofia, Iona smiled at her own fond holiday memories.

There was something about Christmas that just brought out the best in people. That had always been her favorite time of year and she was determined it would be again. He stood up and held his hand out to her.

"I'm Josh," he said.

"Iona," she replied. "What are we going to decorate?"

"How does Santa's sleigh sound?" Josh asked.

Sofia made a face and Iona wondered what it might be like for the six-year-old to be explaining all the time that she didn't believe in Santa. "Well, we've been eyeing the gingerbread men and women. I think Sofia wanted to make a special one for her daddy."

"Even better. Come on over here, ladies, and I'll help you get started."

Sofia smiled up at Iona. "Thanks. I do want to make something special, for Papa."

"I figured you did," she said, ruffling the little girl's hair as they walked to the table. They were both given aprons, gloves and Iona had a twinge of conscience remembering how she'd stuck her hand in the candies earlier, but she was scrupulously clean and had used hand sanitizer, so she felt a little better.

She and Sofia finished making their gingerbread people. And as she decorated her boy, she made sure he had black eyes like her brother and the same dark hair, which she formed from licorice. The both of them were trying to figure out what was next and as the older sister, Iona knew she should be the one to make the first move.

When she was done, she noticed that Sofia was still working, so she decided she'd make another set of gingerbread people to resemble Santa and Mrs. Claus. She thought they'd turned out pretty good. She glanced over at Sofia's creations and noticed she'd made the boy look like her dad, with bright-blue eyes and dark-chocolate hair, and she had made a tie around his neck. The girl also had dark-chocolate hair but it was shorted than Sofia's and had curls on the forehead. The girl had on an apron made of orange frosting and brown eyes.

"I love your cookies. Is that you and your Papa?"

Sofia shook her head. "That's my mama. Even though she's in heaven, Papa misses her."

Iona's heart broke as she looked down at the little girl and she wondered if her path had crossed with Mads', not for business, but to help this little family find the magic of Christmas. Maybe she'd been blown into their lives like the wind in the Candied Apple Café storefront. It made her smile to think she could do that. Her father had always said her faith in people would be her downfall and it had taken her partnership with Cici and Hayley to make her see how wrong he was. Of course, she'd only had the courage to try it because he'd had a massive heart attack and she'd wanted to do something to stand out in his eyes and win his approval.

She shook that thought off as Sofia slipped her small hand into Iona's. She realized this little girl was trying to get her father's approval too.

***

Mads wasn't too thrilled with having to take a call now when he'd insisted that Sofia come to the brunch with St. Nick, but this call wasn't one he could ignore.

Wayne, the duty manager at the Common, texted him that it was urgent, so he called her as he kept an eye on his daughter and Iona.

26

"Sir, we have a major emergency in the retail shop. There is a leak in the ceiling. I've called maintenance and the Duty Manager is taking care of the guests but maintenance think a pipe might have burst. We might need to vacate the rooms above and we're at full occupancy tonight," Wayne said.

"Is the concierge calling other resorts?" Mads asked.

"The concierge can't find rooms due to the tree lighting at Rockefeller Center later. He suggested maybe you could call in some favors."

Mads knew that Lexi had made the right call. "I will. Have the concierge text me the list of who he has been in contact with and I'll start calling in favors."

In the hotel business, there was no such thing as a hands-off management style approach.

"I will," he said. "Is there anything else I can do?"

"I need you to go and check out the rooms and see which, if any, are affected. How many rooms did maintenance think would need to be cleared?" Mads asked.

"They were vague. Housekeeping and the front desk manager are going from room to room to see where the leak started. We believe it shouldn't be more than four rooms on the corner above the retail shop, but they aren't sure how high up the leak is."

"Keep me posted," he said. "I'll drop by later this morning unless you need me there now?"

"I've got this under control. We really need your connections to get rooms for our displaced guests," Wayne said.

"I'll be in touch." He took a moment to make sure that Sofia was still doing okay with Iona and then went to one of the round tables that were set up for families once they'd gotten food from the buffet, after they finished visiting Santa or decorating cookies.

He used the list that the concierge had given him and started making calls. Work was a distraction and he gladly threw himself into it. He'd gambled on staying in Manhattan this Christmas. His brother had suggested they come to California and stay with him, but he knew that running away this year would mean that Sofia would have to deal with Christmas here next year.

He left a message for a friend with a lot of connections in the Manhattan hotel business, and had just set his phone down, when he heard the sound of jingle bells. He glanced up to see Sofia and Iona standing there. Sofia had on a big smile. One of the biggest he'd seen in a long time.

"Papa, we made gingerbread cookies," she said, as she set the cookies on the table in front of him and then climbed up onto his lap.

He glanced down at the cookies and then back at his daughter, who was kicking her leg and swinging it while talking to Iona. He wasn't listening to the conversation, instead he simply saw the cookies and knew that she'd made her mom and him.

His heart was breaking a little bit when he saw them. The fear that lingered in the back of his mind was that he wasn't enough to be both mother and father to his daughter.

"I hope you don't mind," Iona said, sitting down next to him and turning to face him. The bells on the end of her hat jingled, which he noted made Sofia smile.

"I'm sorry, I missed that last bit," he said.

"I let Sofia eat some of the candies while we were decorating, is that okay?"

"Yes, of course," he said, noticing that she watched him carefully. "Sorry, I was distracted, we have an emergency at the Common. We're going to have to head over there soon."

"I don't mind, Papa," Sofia said. "I didn't want to come."

"I remember," Mads said.

"But I'm glad I did," Sofia said. "Thank you, Iona, for helping me with my cookies."

"You're welcome, sweetie," Iona said. "I'll leave you both to it, then. I'd better go find my mom and see if she needs me to do anything."

There was something in her tone that made him wonder if

28

there was more to Iona than long legs, business savvy, and an easy smile. Which was silly because he knew there was. But she'd seemed so carefree about the holidays until this moment.

"I hope your hotel problem is sorted out easily. "I'm sure I'll see you both around," Iona said, walking away from them. He heard Sofia sigh as Iona left.

"What's the matter, imp?"

"I miss her. She's fun."

And fun was what had been in short supply for the two of them for a good long while.

***

The invitation to attend a party at a friend's with offices across from Rockefeller Plaza, who was hosting a tree- lighting party, was something that he'd normally decline. But he'd had to spend the majority of the Saturday at the Common and since Jessie had the day off Sofia had to as well.

It had been a long day for them both and the tree lighting would be something festive before they had to head back home. Sofia had been inspired by her cookie decorating at the Santa Brunch and when the Common's pastry chef had offered her some round sugar cookies and a colored icing to keep her entertained, she'd eagerly jumped at the chance.

She had made seven cookies all for her friends. She'd decorated them all to look like the friend she was gifting the cookie to. One of them had red hair, blue eyes, and a Santa cap on its head.

"Who is that one for?"

"Iona. Since she lives in our building I thought I'd drop it off to her."

"We don't know her apartment," Mads pointed out.

"You can text her," Sofia said.

"I'll do that later. Do you want to go to a party tonight? We'd be able to see the tree lighting at Rockefeller Plaza," he said.

"Sure," she said. "What about my cookies?"

"We can go home and get changed first," he said.

They went home and Sofia darted into her bedroom to get changed and Mads changed his sweater but then got distracted by texts from the duty manager that he had to respond to.

Sofia came back into the living room dressed in jeans and a thick sweater that had been one of the last things Gill had purchased for their daughter. It was getting a little short in the sleeves but Sofia didn't want to give it up and Mads had found that he couldn't make her.

"Grab your coat, Sof." She did so, wrapping her scarf around her neck before she reached for her coat.

Mads took it from her and held it so she could slip her arms in easily and then stooped down in front of his daughter to fasten the coat and then adjust her scarf.

"We should invite Iona to join us," Sofia said out of the blue.

He didn't know how to react to that. Encouraging a friendship with someone he was doing business with didn't seem like a wise idea. If they ran into her, that was one thing.

"I don't think so," he said.

She got that stubborn look on her face. "Why not?"

"I am in the middle of a business deal with her, so it's probably best that we keep some distance from her."

"Why?"

"If the deal goes south … don't worry about it. That's my job," Mads said.

"Okay, Papa," she said, going over to the hall table where a framed picture of Gill was, Sofia touched her fingers to her lips, kissed them and then touched Gill's face. "Bye, Mama."

Mads put his hand on his daughter's back, holding open the door for her as they exited their apartment in a nice building on Manhattan's Upper East Side. The night had already started to darken and there was a light fall of snow beyond the windows of the lobby. The piped Christmas music was nearly drowned out by the sound of conversations and Sofia slipped her hand into his as they walked toward the doors.

He glanced around the lobby, telling himself he wasn't looking for Iona but disappointed all the same that it was empty. Sofia sang along with the radio that his driver had on. The next song to come on was Michael Bublé's version of "Santa Claus is Coming to Town".

He glanced at Sofia, who had started singing, and then stopped and he knew he had to get to the bottom of this Santa thing. But how?

He started to sing along. His voice was rusty because it had been a long time since he'd done any singing, but he remembered Gill always loved Christmas carols. Sofia glanced over at him.

"Do you like this song?"

"I do. Remember, Mommy liked it too," he said.

Sofia tipped her head to the side. "She loved singing."

"Especially with you," Mads added. It had been one of the things that Gill's illness hadn't been able to take from her.

As the song switched to the second verse, he started to sing again and Sofia joined in. When the song ended, she didn't say anything but Mads felt … like he'd done the right thing. They arrived at the building where the party was and as they exited their car he noticed Iona was speaking to the security guard at the door.

Her red hair was down, hanging around her shoulders and she had on a camel-colored coat. She smiled when she noticed them.

"Hello, Erikssons," Iona said. "What are you two doing tonight?"

"We are here for the tree lighting," Sofia said.

"One of my frat brothers has an office in this building and invited us to a party tonight."

"Who?" Iona asked.

"Jeff Miller," Mads said.

"I'm going to the same party. His wife and I went to the Dalton School together. She and I go way back," Iona said. The security guard cleared Iona and she stepped inside the lobby but waited for them.

It only took a minute for him and Sofia to be cleared by security. The three of them walked together to the elevators.

"I love the tree lighting. Two years ago, I went with my friends Hayley and Cici and we stood outside in the cold and it was so crowded. I decided to skip it last year, but Blaire's party seems like it will be fun."

Mads realized he was staring at Iona, but he had just realized how pretty she was. Earlier, he'd been concentrating on business, on work, *that* had been his salvation, but now that he had a moment in the elevator to just look at her, he couldn't stop staring. Her skin sort of glistened and it was almost as if she'd channeled the magic of the season into her appearance somehow.

"We've never been to see it, but Sofia likes trees."

"Do you?" Iona asked, looking down at his daughter.

Mads watched her, trying to see the sadness that Sofia had glimpsed earlier but he didn't see it. Instead, he just saw a woman who was smiling and enjoying the holiday season.

"I do. I have a collection of tiny crystal ones that Papa has brought me back from all over the world," Sofia said.

"That's so sweet. Which one is your favorite?" Iona asked.

"I think the one from Spain. Do you know the one, Papa?"

"The Lladro one of Mommy's, right?" It was one he'd purchased for Gill before Sofia had been born. It was a scene with a Christmas tree and a couple exchanging gifts in front of it. It was the one that had started Sofia's collection.

"Yes. It's so pretty, Iona," Sofia said. "You can come and see it sometime."

"I'd like that." "Christmas is my favorite time of year," she said.

"Why is that?" Mads asked.

"I like how everything is lit up with bright colors and how people seem to smile more easily. But mostly I like that time slows down," Iona said. "When I was your age, Sofia, it was the one time during the year that my family were all together. Dad didn't travel and we just spent more time together."

Sofia looked up at him. "Like us."

"Just like us," Mads agreed. As much as he wanted this holiday to be over, he was very aware that Sofia was only six and he wanted her memories of Christmas to be good ones.

"I'm glad to hear that," Iona said.

He took Sofia's hand as they exited the elevator and since it was an office building, they stepped into an open area where they could hear the music and voices near the windows that overlooked the Plaza.

Jeff came over as soon as he saw them.

"Mads, good to see you," he said, holding out his hand.

Mads shook it and then Jeff scooped Sofia up and gave her a hug. "How's my favorite kiddo?"

"Good," Sofia said. "I've been decorating cookies today."

"You have? My mom used to say you could eat the broken ones," Jeff told her.

"Well, I ate the decorations," she said with a giggle.

Jeff put her down and turned to Iona.

"Hello, Io. I didn't realize you two knew each other," Jeff said.

"Hiya. The Common is interested in a partnership with the Candied Apple Café."

"Hmm. Sounds interesting. Your dad would be impressed," Jeff said, leading them into the party.

"I hope so," Iona said.

"Of course, he would be," Mads said. "The Candied Apple Café is one of the best-run businesses in this town."

"Thanks," she said with a smile, and then Blair came over and the two women started talking.

They were separated and he watched her go. He knew that

business was the only relationship they had, but something about Iona made it hard for him to forget that.

Chapter 4

The first-time Iona and Blair had met they'd been in second grade and both of them were trying to be the top student in the class. Both were strong type-A personalities who had lived up to their potential. Her father hadn't been impressed and it had only spurred Iona to work harder.

Blair and Jeff had been married for eighteen months and her friend seemed happy. She had started to cut back hours at the magazine where she worked as a feature editor and Blair had told her in confidence that Jeff wanted to start a family.

"Is there a reason why we are in the corner?" Iona asked. "Are you pregnant?"

"What? No. I mean, I don't think so. I won't know for a few more days," she said. "I dragged you over here to ask about Mads. Are you *with* him?"

"No," Iona said. "We just arrived at the same time."

"Okay," Blair said.

"He is cute, though," Iona said. There was no denying it. The dark-blue button-down shirt he wore made it impossible for her to stop looking at his eyes. And his thick black hair begged for her to run her fingers through it. She knew that she'd never do it.

Mads and Sofia were complicated and she was busy. The Candied Apple Café didn't leave any time for a social life. And the few times she'd tried … well it hadn't gone well.

"He is. But he's complicated, Io," Blair said. "His wife died last year, just days after Christmas."

"I know," Iona said. She would have guessed that he had some sort of tragedy in his past, even if he hadn't told her about his wife. There was an aura of sadness around him at times. He was talking with a group of men and she noticed he kept his eye on Sofia, who had drifted off with a group of children.

"I just don't want to see you get hurt," Blair said. "I mean that matchmaker business and everything. How are things with Theo?"

Iona took a sip of her chocolatini before she answered. "Good. Well, awkward but good. Nico is really perfect for Theo and despite the fun we had together over the summer, there wasn't any real passion between us. I mean, I only said yes to the matchmaker because of my mom."

"And the fact that your dad is gone," Blair said.

Iona shrugged. "Maybe … but really, it was more that everyone I know is getting married and settling down and I don't have time to date so I thought it'd be a short cut."

"Fair enough. If Jeff hadn't been so persistent I probably wouldn't be married to him either," Blair said.

They both laughed at that. Jeff had fallen hard for her friend the moment he'd laid eyes on her and hadn't given up, despite the fact that Blair had refused to accept a date with him for two years.

Jeff gestured for Blair to join him and Iona moved on to socialize with another group but noticed that Sofia was sitting on the floor by herself. She faced the plate glass floor-to-ceiling windows that offered a view of the plaza and the massive dark shape of the tree that would have its lights turned on shortly.

Ditching her martini glass on the tray of a passing waiter, she made her way over to the little girl.

"Can I join you?" Iona asked.

"Sure," Sofia said.

"Tell me about your tree collection," Iona said as she sat down.

"It's really not that big but I have six so far. One for each Christmas. When I was two Mommy got sick and we couldn't have a real tree."

Iona hadn't wanted to pry into Mads' personal life and realized now that Sofia was telling her things that he might not want her to. "My brother is allergic to animals so we could never have a pet when I was growing up. My mom got me a large pink stuffed dog that I called Fluffy."

"Papa says we travel too much for a dog," Sofia said with more maturity than her years.

Just then *Must Be Santa* by Bob Dylan came on and Iona, whose mom loved Dylan, started to sing along, which made Sofia laugh and clap her hands. The music was catchy and the song had a lot of call and response, so soon they were both singing along, laughing. It was just a silly song and then in the middle there was a harmonica solo, which was fun.

This was what she loved most about the holidays, how a song could just lift the spirits. And she saw that Sofia was smiling the same way.

A deep tenor joined in and Iona looked up as Mads joined them, sitting down on the other side of Sofia. Sofia stopped singing along and watched Mads. Iona didn't stop singing, just winked at Mads, who nodded at her. Sofia leaned into the curve of her father's body and clapped her hands along with the song until it ended.

"That's a funny song," Sofia said.

"It is."

She was a stranger to this family. A business partner, at best, and now that the little girl had her father with her, Iona should get up and leave.

Really, she should.

But she couldn't.

She made small talk with the people that Mads introduced her to and she'd brought some Candied Apple Café business cards to hand out. But she didn't really feel like working the room tonight. Instead her mind was focused on that little girl who had been singing until her father sat down. Mads doted on Sofia, so Iona doubted he would have cautioned her to stop.

That meant something else was at play here. Something that was none of her business, she reminded herself again. Blair had said that he was complicated. Iona knew that, but something about him kept her here. She wanted to help him. Wanted to … know him better.

"It's almost time for the tree lighting," Jeff announced. "Sofia, come over here with the other kids so you have a good spot to view it."

She got to her feet and ran over to Jeff, who took her hand and led her to the other children. Iona knew she should get up and join the others, but Mads didn't seem to be ready to get up so she stayed there.

"Why do you think Sofia stopped singing when I joined you?" Mads asked.

"Maybe she just wanted to listen to your voice," Iona said. "She was watching you."

"I know. She's been so … I don't know what to do this holiday season. Gill used to sing songs with her all the time and I never wanted to intrude on that. You know, it was their thing. I just don't want her hurt. Songs don't hurt, in fact they usually cheer her up."

"I'm sorry. I really don't know what to tell you to do," Iona said. "My own relationship with my dad was complicated. I think you and Sofia are figuring it out."

"I hope so. Thanks for giving me an outsider's perspective. I've been so focused on Sofia and making sure that her mom's death doesn't dominate her childhood."

Iona felt like she was on the cusp of being more than a business associate to Mads. She could just smile and get up and leave or she could ask more questions and really try to help this little duo out.

"When did her mom die?" Iona asked gently. It wasn't in her nature to not ask questions.

"December 27th," he said flatly. His voice had gone cold and his eyes were that icy blue again.

Iona scooted closer and hugged him. He held himself stiffly in her embrace and she sighed. "I'm so sorry."

"Me too," he admitted, his arms coming around her briefly and then they dropped.

But their eyes met and he didn't look away. He tipped his head to the side and she sat there waiting. Normally, she would be the aggressor, but nothing with Mads was normal. He wrapped a strand of her hair around his finger and then pulled his hand back. Leaning in, his lips brushed hers so lightly that she almost felt like she'd imagined it. Except for the shivers of awareness sliding down her spine.

"Papa!"

He pulled back, getting to his feet as Sofia joined them.

"Papa, come on. You're going to miss the tree!"

He turned away from Iona and she stood there watching him walk away with his daughter.

***

Keeping his eyes off of Iona was proving a problem for Mads as the evening wore on. He knew he had no business kissing her and his rational mind hadn't been a part of that decision. It had been pure instinct. It had been a long time since he'd felt anything around a woman or really even noticed one. But Iona wasn't the kind of woman who could be ignored. Something that many of the other men in the room were noticing.

She was easy to talk to and laughed frequently. She had come over to Sofia and him right after the tree lighting and posed with them for a photo. "There we go. You can add this to your tree collection, Sofia."

"Oh, thank you," Sofia said. "I heard there are cookies … Papa?"

"Go and get one," he said, ruffling her hair and she ran off to the table with the large cookies on it. He watched his daughter as she carefully walked along the table checking out all of the offerings before making her selection.

"This was a lot of fun, but I've got an early meeting, so I'm going to head out soon."

"No problem. Sofia really likes you. You make her laugh and that is something she hasn't done a lot lately," he said. But he didn't want to keep talking about his daughter; he wanted to know more about Iona. "I have heard a lot about your father from Jeff. He mentioned that he was impetus for you to start your own business."

Iona blushed and shook her head. "You asked about me?"

"Well, Jeff volunteered," Mads said.

"It's okay. Jeff does business with Summerlin Industries so he knew my dad pretty well."

"That explains why he brought it up. I guess it wasn't an easy relationship," Mads said. He wasn't going to push it but he'd told her more about his personal life than he'd meant to.

"No, it wasn't. He pushed me hard and never really gave me a compliment … that I needed him to do."

Mads put his hand on Iona's shoulder to comfort her but he admitted to himself that it was also because he liked touching her. "You're entitled to want your dad to say you did a good job."

She tilted her head to the side. "So true. But he's gone now so I probably should get over it."

"If only we could tell ourselves that and make it happen."

"Sorry, I forgot that you have …"

"Don't do that. Don't belittle what you're feeling," he said. So many times over the last year he knew his friends had pulled back from him, afraid to share anything because of his grief.

"It's just compared to what you've lost, my thing isn't a big deal."

Mads had heard that before. Many of his friends had stopped calling and dropping by when Gill had first gotten sick and then distanced themselves even more after her death. It was as if they didn't know how to act around him anymore.

"I'm glad you feel that it isn't a big deal," he said. "No one should have to feel what I did. And you know I'm not judging you for having fun or not grieving. One of the hardest things for me to accept was that life moves on."

"How do you mean?" Iona asked.

"Just that the world didn't stop when Gill exited it. Sofia had school to go to. I had meetings to focus on. It was like Gill was gone but everything else kept moving forward and at first I wanted to stop too," Mads said.

He didn't want to analyze why he was telling Iona so much of this stuff. But honestly, it felt good to talk to someone who hadn't known Gill or him back then. He didn't feel like he had to couch his words to protect the family they'd been. Sofia is the reason I get up each day."

She reached over and squeezed his upper arm in sympathy. "She's a very good reason to stay motivated. I have my partnership in the Candied Apple Café and, for me, that's reward enough."

He noticed her smile when she mentioned her friends and he envied her that close relationship. He had Sofia, of course, but he and his brother had drifted apart over time and he'd stopped trying with his friends when Gill had gotten sick.

Iona's watch pinged and she looked down at it. "I really do have to go. I enjoyed talking to you tonight."

"Me too," he said. I think we'll call it a night as well. We can share a ride home?" Mads asked.

"Thank you," she responded.

She waited while he got Sofia and the three of them left together. Jeff and Blair came over to give Sofia a gift bag and he thought he saw concern in their eyes.

He felt that twinge of guilt at the thought he was forgetting Gill. He'd never thought he'd feel any real emotion towards another woman, but he liked Iona, remembered when he'd almost kissed her and knew he wanted more than a brief brush of lips. *Maybe more than liked her.*

***

Sunday was for lazing around in bed and Iona had enjoyed that very much. She had partially decorated her Christmas tree, meaning she'd gotten the lights on and then had spent the rest of the day sitting around in sweatpants, binge- watching all the Santa Clause movies and trying to dwell on Mads. *He'd almost kissed her.* That brief brush of lips had intrigued her. Awoken something she'd ignored pretty successfully for years. Heck, she'd even been willing to have a passionless marriage with Nico before everything had shifted and they'd both realized why there was no passion between them at all.

She felt like a bit of a slug by six p.m. Forcing herself to take a shower and put on clothes and make-up, she texted Cici and Hayley to see if they wanted to go out for dinner.

Can't tonight. Holly, Hoop and I are on our way back from the Hamptons, Cici texted.

Then Hayley replied. *Ugh. I wish I could but I have to get in extra early tomorrow to finish up our special truffle box. I want you both there early as well.*

She texted back with emojis since *Wah, why won't my friends come out and play with me?* wasn't very adult. She could order in. But she hadn't left the house all day.

She decided she'd go to Korali Estiatorio on Third and pick up spanakopita for dinner. She opened her door just as someone was knocking and looked down to see little Sofia standing there.

"Hello," Iona said, surprised. "What are you doing here?"

"I wanted to bring you something I made for you," Sofia said, holding up a small pastry box with the Common logo on it.

"Thank you," Iona said gratefully, taking it from her. She glanced down the hall and saw a woman in her twenties only a few feet away.

"Hi, I'm Iona," she said to the woman.

"Jessie. I'm this scamp's nanny."

"I was on my way out," she said. She'd pretty much decided last night that she needed to steer clear of Sofia and her too-cute father. She had lot of big plans and only by focusing on them was she going to achieve them. She'd learned a lot from her father's example.

"That's okay, we can't stay," Jessie said. "But she wanted to make sure you got her gift today."

"Want me to open it now?"

Sofia nodded. It was really hard for her to keep her distance like she knew she should. She liked Sofia. Saw a little bit of herself in the lonely little girl. Though she'd had Theo, he'd been the golden child and everyone had adored him and Iona had always felt isolated.

She stooped down so she was on eye level with Sofia and then opened the box. The cookie was decorated in her image and made her smile.

"Thank you, sweetie. I love it."

"You're welcome."

"Okay, scamp, let's go. We're under strict orders to get right back," Jessie said.

From Mads.

He was probably of the same mindset that encouraging a friendship between her and his daughter wasn't a good idea. But

Sofia clearly needed something from her. Iona made up her mind to resolve the business issue as soon as possible.

"Better get back, then," Iona said.

"It's just 'cause he has to get back to the hotel," Sofia said.

Iona remembered his call at the brunch and imagined that running the hotel took up a lot of his time. Yet he did seem to manage being with Sofia as well.

"Maybe we will run into each other again," Iona said, stepping into the hall and closing her door.

"I'm sure we will," Sofia said. "Bye."

Jessie and Sofia walked down the hall in the opposite direction of the elevators and Iona was tempted to turn and watch them, hoping again for a glimpse of Mads, but instead she forced herself to keep walking.

Eye on the prize.

Her father's voice echoed through her mind. He'd been a great one for dishing out advice and well-meaning "honesty" about ways she could improve herself at in her role at work. She worked longer and harder than anyone else on her marketing team at Summerlin Industries and never had he acknowledged it. Just told her how good Theo was doing in his role as COO. Even finding a way to turn the long hours she spent at the office into her trying to avoid dating and finding a man.

Iona paused in the lobby.

She hadn't realized how much of that anger she still carried around towards her father. He'd been gone for over two years now. She missed him, but a part of her acknowledged that she wanted him to still be here to see her successes. But would she have had the courage to leave Summerlin Industries if he'd still been alive?

She stepped out of her building into the brisk December night and inhaled the cold air, tipping her head back to see that the sky was cloudless. It was so clear, she imagined that if she wasn't in the city she might be able to make out the stars.

The door to the building opened, she stepped out of the path of the person glancing over her shoulder and meeting the icy-gray gaze of Mads.

"Iona."

"Mads."

"Are you going in?"

"No," she said. "Heading to dinner. Sofia mentioned you were heading back to the hotel."

"Yes. We have a leak above our retail shop. Turns out the problem is bigger than originally believed and I have to get down there to soothe one of our longtime guests."

"Good luck. If you'd like I can send a basket of Candied Apple goodies over in the morning for any of your displaced guests," she said. The gesture would be a nice promo opportunity.

"That would be a nice touch. Thank you."

"No problem. Just text me the number of baskets needed and the guest names."

"Thanks," he said. She nodded and took a step away from him, but he caught her arm in his hand.

She stopped and half turned toward him. Their eyes met and he closed the gap between them.

"I told myself this was a bad idea, but I can't stop wondering what it would be like to kiss you," he said.

She just leaned in the slightest bit, their lips met and a tingle spread down her neck through her body. His lips were firm but soft and parted against hers. She felt the warmth of his breath in her mouth and then the brush of his tongue over hers. She reached up, grabbing onto the lapels of his coat to steady herself.

She opened her eyes and shifted back from him. He just traced his finger over his mouth, then nodded. "Good evening."

He walked away and she watched him leave. Blair's comment from the night before ran through her mind. Iona had thought she understood what "complicated" meant, but she really hadn't.

Chapter 5

"Iona?"

She shook her head to clear it, forced a smile and looked over at Cici. "Sorry, what were you saying?" Iona asked.

Cici looked tired, as was to be expected since she had a two-week-old baby, but also glowy … was that even a word? But she did. Also Cici looked happy. Happier than Iona had ever seen her. She was getting ready to celebrate so much in her life.

"I was just inviting you to a dinner party on Saturday evening."

"Should you be entertaining already?"

"Well, if you must know Hoop's friend Alfonso is giving us an evening of cooking as an early wedding present and he said to invite our closest friends and that includes you."

"Of course, I'll be there."

Cici blushed, nibbled her lower lip, cleared her throat and then finally just sighed. "Should I put you down as one or will you be bringing someone?"

This was exactly why she had wanted the matchmaking to work out. Everyone else in their circle was paired up. In the past she could have invited Theo along, but now he had a partner too. "Put me down for two. I'll find someone to bring along."

"I will, you know it's fine if it's just you. It really is going to just be our closest friends ... in fact Xavier — you remember him? He works with Garrett on the force ... he's single and he'll be there," Cici said.

She shook her head. Xavier was still in love with his ex-wife. Anyone who'd spent ten minutes talking to him could easily see that. Xavier was a detective who worked with Hayley's fiancé and had been divorced for a year. "You should invite his ex. He still loves her."

"Really?"

"Yes. He did nothing but talk about her at the cook-out that Garrett and Hayley had at Labor Day weekend."

"Interesting. I think he has two kids. Maybe I'll suggest we make it family-friendly," Cici said. "But that still leaves us stuck for someone for you."

"I said I'd bring someone," Iona said firmly. "And I will."

"Okay," Cici said, reaching across the small table and putting her hand on Iona's. "I was hoping that things would have worked out with Nico."

"Me too," she said. Cici and Hoop had gone on her first date with the Greek millionaire.

"Are you two having fun without me?" Hayley said, coming from the back of the store and her candy kitchen.

"I thought you were in the kitchen concocting greatness," Iona replied.

Hayley's blonde hair had grown out since last January, when she'd shorn it all off, and it now brushed her shoulders. She had on a pair of leggings and a thick tunic sweater. "As a matter of fact, I had a genius idea for a new truffle that I have made some samples of. And I need your opinions."

Hayley put a small plate on the table between the three of them. There were six truffles lined up in white, milk, and dark chocolate.

"Ooo ... what's inside?" Cici asked.

"I don't want to say, but I'm calling it Christmas Morning,"

Hayley said. "I'm not sure which one works the best: white, milk, or dark. All opinions are welcome. I have a batch ready for the staff to try and rank as well."

There were times like this when Iona almost had to pinch herself at the success they'd made of their little candy shop. It had started as an idea they'd had and grown into so much more than she'd expected. She listened to her two friends talking and closed her eyes for a moment to thank God for the blessed life she had.

"Iona, which one do you want to try first?" Hayley asked.

"Which one do you recommend?" Iona asked her friend.

"Knowing your tastes run to dark and spicy, I'd say you should try the dark one first. Cici, definitely milk for you."

They ate chocolate and chatted about the truffles and Iona reminded herself that her life was full as it was. Hers was hectic and busy, but that didn't stop her from thinking about Mads at odd moments. And what had the kiss been about last night?

She'd tried not to dwell on it; it was only a kiss after all, but it didn't seem that way today. As she left the candy shop, walking home toward her apartment on the Upper East Side she couldn't help but remember Mads and the look in his eyes when he'd lifted his head.

A little zing went through her. The snow was lightly falling as she entered her building and she smiled at the doorman, who wished her good evening.

Then she thought about little Sofia, who was struggling to figure out what she believed in and find her way this holiday season, remembering how Mads was unsure if he was doing a good job.

Complicated.

***

Sofia wasn't in the mood to be cooperative on Tuesday morning and Mads was running out of patience. He tried to be even-tempered and to give his daughter a break most of the time but she was being a little bit bratty this morning. Jessie's fever had returned overnight so Mads was on dad duty, which was one of his favorite things. *Normally.*

But he hadn't slept well last night; fevered dreams of Iona had kept him awake. He had some outside plumbers coming to the Common to evaluate the leak at nine and he'd hoped to get there before they did. But something was up with his daughter.

She hadn't wanted to eat her breakfast and then when he'd put away the muffins that he'd set out originally, she'd changed her mind. But by then he was losing patience with her and told her she'd have to have cereal. Which she had taken her time selecting from the four choices in the pantry. Then he'd had to stand over her while she slowly ate every bit of the cereal she'd insisted she wanted.

Now she couldn't leave for school unless she had two French braids.

"What's wrong with one braid?" Mads asked.

"Papa, I wore my hair that way yesterday. And today it has to be two."

Mads was looking down at the top of his daughter's head, completely unsure what to do. He was tempted to go and see if Jessie felt well enough to braid Sofia's hair, but she'd been pale when he'd dosed her up with ibuprofen so he was on his own. He also had contractors coming at eight-thirty, by which time Sofia would be late for school.

"Sof, I don't know if I can do it."

"You can, Papa. You're a problem-solver," she said.

True.

"That's right, I am," he said, lifting her off her feet and nuzzling a kiss against the top of her head. He'd do this and maybe figure out what was going on with Sofia at the same time.

"Did you Google it?" he asked.

"I did," she said.

She held up her tablet and he glanced down. It was just braiding, right? Gill had shown him the basics when they both had realized that her illness wasn't going to go away and one day he'd have to do this. He brushed Sofia's dark curly hair, which made it frizz out around her head, and Sofia started laughing and he had to chuckle as well when he looked down at her.

"How's that? Want to go to school looking like this?"

"Papa, you're too silly."

"I know," he said and read the instructions and then started working on the braids. They were uneven from the top side, but they were done.

"Thanks!"

"You're welcome. Are you ready to go?" he asked.

"Just gotta grab my bag … oh, and there was a note for you," she said, digging in her bag.

This time of year, there were all kinds of notes coming home from school, so he was expecting to see a copied note to the entire class, not a handwritten notecard addressed to him.

"What is this?"

She shrugged but looked guilty. "I don't know. And we have to go or we will be late."

He opened the envelope as she urged him out of their apartment and toward the elevator.

He glanced down at the first line of the note.

"You were *fighting*?"

"Not really."

"Not really? Sof, this note says otherwise."

"It was about Santa."

Mads sighed. He hit the stop button on the elevator. He stooped down to eye level with his daughter. "What happened?"

"Remy said that maybe I was naughty and that's why Santa doesn't come to me," Sofia said.

"What did you say to that?" Mads asked.

She heaved a big sigh. "I'm not naughty."

"What happened next?" Because as responsible as this all sounded, he had a note in his hand that stated it was more than a conversation.

"He said *Of course you'd say that.*"

Sofia looked down at the floor of the elevator car.

"Then?" Mads prompted.

"I told him I'm not naughty, just smart, and that's probably what was confusing for him," Sofia said. "He laughed at that and said something mean so I just … I kicked him, Papa. And then he said he barely felt my kick so I kicked him again even harder and that's when Miss Pembroke came over."

"Sofia," Mads said, drawing his daughter into his arms. "Did he hit or kick you?"

"No. He said he's not allowed to hit girls," Sofia said.

"That's good. You shouldn't hit boys, or anyone, for that matter. Did you apologize?" he asked.

"No. I don't feel bad about kicking him," Sofia admitted. "He's not a very nice boy."

"Then don't talk or play with him," Mads said. "You're going to have to apologize."

"I know," she said.

"Is that why you've been so difficult this morning?"

She nodded. He hugged her close to him. He hated that she had gotten into an argument. But there were going to be people who didn't agree with her throughout her life so she probably needed to get used to dealing with conflict.

"I think we are supposed to stop by the principal's office this morning," he said.

"We are. But if you have to get to work I'll let them know," she said, twisting her hands together.

He pulled his phone out and texted the duty manager, who could handle the meeting until he got there. "I don't. Nothing's more important than you," he said.

51

"I'm sorry, Papa."

"It's okay, Sof. Do you think maybe we should talk more about Santa?" he asked.

She put her hand on the side of his face like she did sometimes and looked him in the eyes. "No, Papa. We both know that miracles don't exist."

His heart broke wide open. She was so small, so young. He wished Sofia could still believe in miracles.

He scooped her up and hugged her close. He was doing the best he could and there were times when he really felt like he had no clue what he was doing at all.

It wasn't a feeling he liked. And he knew he was never going to get used to it. He'd expected to raise his daughter with Gill. He'd figured he'd dote on her and spoil her. Not have to second-guess and question every decision he ever made.

The ride to school was filled with bouts of Sofia singing and then going quiet.

"Let's go get this over with," he said as they got out of the car in front of her school.

She slipped her hand into his as they walked into the school. He wanted to make Sofia's life easier for her but he didn't want her to ever think she couldn't share her opinion. And he was proud of her standing up for herself. Up until she kicked the boy.

***

Iona did three press interviews in the morning and then arranged the new Christmas Morning truffles for a photo shoot in the back room. They had a service they used for the catalogue that they sent to their regular customers in the tri-state area but she had found that for the website her photos were just as good as the photographer's. And since she needed something else on her plate to justify avoiding her mom and her brother, it made sense to take on more work.

Iona was upstairs where they held classes for couples who wanted to learn to make truffles. She had just about finished up when she heard footsteps on the stairs.

"Someone is here to see you," Cici said from the doorway.

"Who?"

"Me," Sofia said, stepping around Cici. "You remember Jessie?"

Jessie looked like the walking dead. Pale skin, red nose and she moved gingerly into the room. She seemed well medicated against whatever it was that had made her sick, but also tired. She was watching Sofia like someone who was afraid to let her guard down.

"Do you want to have a seat, Jessie?" Iona asked. "How about something hot to drink? We are famous for our cocoa, but you look like you could use a cup of tea."

"I could. But we're not supposed to be here and Sofia knows it. But she insisted," Jessie said. "And she has a good reason, so I'll just sit over here. Be quick, girly."

Sofia nodded, then hurried to Iona's side.

"Iona, I need your help. I got into a fight at school."

She went down on her knee, putting her hand on Sofia's shoulder. "Are you okay?"

"Yes. I'm fine. I'm the one who kicked someone. Anyway, I need to apologize — even though I'm really not sorry …"

"Sofia," Jessie said. "We've been over this. You have to write a note."

Iona glanced at Jessie. She wanted more details but she could get them later. "How can I help?"

"Well, I wanted to see if I could get a box of candy to go along with my note," Sofia said.

"Sure. Jessie, why don't you wait for us in the Café area? I'm going to have Nick bring you a cup of tea and I'll help Sofia pick out a box of chocolates."

"Great. But our driver will be back in …" Jessie glanced down at her watch, "ten minutes, so make it quick."

"We will," Sofia said, slipping her hand into Iona's.

Iona led the way down the stairs into the retail section. "What is this person like? Was it a boy or a girl?"

Sofia slipped her hand from Iona's and walked over to the display boxes. "A boy. One who isn't very smart and is mean. Do you have any chocolates like that?"

Iona had to hide her smile. "No. We don't. Surely there is something that's not awful about him. What's his name?"

"Remy LeBeau."

There was a note in Sofia's voice that didn't sound like anger. "Do you like him?"

"He said I was naughty, so I can't like him now," she said to Iona.

"Why would he say that? Because you kicked him?" Iona asked.

"No. Because I said Santa doesn't visit me," she said. "Papa said I can't tell kids that he isn't real. He said they had to figure it out on their own."

She agreed with Mads on that front. But she had to wonder if he was happy about the fact that his daughter was getting into fights because of her beliefs about St. Nick. She guessed he wasn't. But that wasn't any of her business.

Chocolate was.

Iona looked around the retail shop when she had an idea. "Come with me into the kitchen."

She held Sofia's hand as they walked through the crowded shop and into the kitchen. Hayley was still working on her creations and overseeing her staff as they assembled the Christmas Morning truffles.

"Hayley, I need you."

"Yes?" her friend asked, coming over and smiling at Sofia. "Hello."

"Hi," Sofia said.

"We need box of truffles for an apology gift; can you help us?"

54

Iona asked.

Hayley raised one eyebrow but didn't ask any questions. "I can. But I need the details. Is the gift for a boy or a girl?"

"A boy ... a *mean* one," Sofia said.

Hayley asked Sofia a few more questions as she moved around the kitchen, picking up different truffles until the box held six chocolates.

"I think he'll like this," Hayley said, handing the box to Sofia.

Iona took Sofia into her office to custom-make a card to go into the box. "Here's a notecard for you to write your apology on."

"Thanks."

Sofia went to the guest table in her office and sat on the floor on her knees to write out the card. She worked over the note slowly and carefully, taking her time with her penmanship, studying her card as she wrote. The concentration in her expression reminded her of Mads.

"Done."

"Great. Let's get your chocolates and I'll tie it up with a ribbon and you and Jessie can head home."

"Thanks," Sofia said.

She took care of everything and then Jessie paid for the chocolates and they left. Iona stood in the doorway watching them leave. Hayley came out in her chef's whites and put her arm around Iona's shoulders. "How do you know that precocious child?"

"Her dad is Mads Eriksson, CEO of the New York Common. She's something else, isn't she?" Iona asked, not wanting to talk about Mads.

"She is. Bet her father is too," Hayley said.

"He is," she admitted. She thought about Sofia and that boy from school calling her naughty. "Hay, can you make a spicy truffle?"

"Yes, why?"

"Well, wouldn't it be fun to have a two-truffle gift box that was 'naughty or nice' themed?"

"I like it. I have some spicy chocolates that have a little bite to them but aren't over the top. How does that sound?"

"Perfect," Iona said. Hayley left to try different pairings and Iona told herself that coming up with a new marketing campaign was satisfying, but she knew that a little bit of it was the warm feeling she'd had when she'd had Sofia in the shop with her. She was starting to like that little family … maybe too much.

Chapter 6

Mads hadn't had the best day, so when he got home at nine after Sofia's bedtime and saw Jessie watching TV in the living room, he wasn't that happy. Bedtime rituals were important to him. But the leak in the hotel wasn't easy to fix and he hadn't been able to get away.

"Hey, Mads. Glad you're home. I put Sofia to bed but she was determined to wait up for you," Jessie said. She still looked pale, but he knew from her text updates that her fever had subsided and she was managing her cold symptoms with over-the-counter medicines. "She might still be awake."

"Thanks. How are you feeling?"

She gave him a weak smile. "Better, but still not one hundred percent."

"I'm glad you're a bit better. I'll go check on Sofia."

"Also, if you didn't eat, we had Indian and I saved some for you."

"Thanks, Jessie," he said. "I am hungry."

"I'll heat it up while you go see Sofia."

He nodded and walked down the hall towards the bedrooms. Sofia's door was propped open a half inch with a doorstopper and he carefully pushed it fully open, walking into the room.

There was a lamp next to her bed that they'd gotten for her nursery. It had a rotating lampshade that projected the cow jumping over the moon and stars onto the wall.

Treading softly, he approached her bed and saw Sofia curled on her side, hugging her dolly, Peaches, sleeping soundly. She looked so sweet with her thick black hair curling around her head. He leaned down and kissed her softly and then drew her covers up over her shoulders before quietly leaving her room.

He went down the hall to his own room and changed into a pair of sweatpants and a tee-shirt. Then he went into the kitchen, where Jessie had left a plate for him. He noticed the box of chocolates on the counter and took his curry with him to check it out. He saw that it had Remy's name on the card.

He ate his dinner and cleaned up before going to find Jessie.

"What did Sofia get for Remy?" he asked.

She turned the volume down on the reality television show she was watching.

"Chocolates. She insisted on stopping by the Candied Apple Café on the way home and I hope you don't mind but I gave in and took her," Jessie said. "She insisted that her friend Iona would help her figure out how to say she was sorry."

He shook his head. He'd been on the receiving end of Sofia's stubbornness and while Jessie usually could resist, she was still getting over being sick. "It's okay. What did she get?"

Jessie smiled. "A box of truffles, but she explained several times that she was doing it under protest."

Mads laughed. That sounded like his daughter. "I'm going to work for a while in my study. Are you sure you're feeling better?"

"I am. I'll be up with Sofia for breakfast and the school run."

"Thanks," Mads said. "I will probably need to be at the Common earlier tomorrow but I want to see her before I leave."

"Okay."

He left her in the living room and went down the hall to his study. He took his smart phone from his pocket and texted a note to Iona, thanking her for helping out Sofia.

She replied straightaway. *No problem. I made sure she included a handwritten card, but I have no idea what she wrote on it. I hope that's okay.*

Yes, it is, he sent back.

His phone vibrated and he saw the call was from Iona.

"Hello?"

"Hi. Sorry to call but I didn't want to text this," she said.

She was going to call him out for kissing her; he didn't blame her. He'd walked away because … that kiss had been too good. He shouldn't have done it.

"I've been invited to a party this weekend and feel free to say no, but I thought maybe you and Sofia would like to come as my guests."

A party with her friends.

"Blair and Jeff?" he asked.

"No. Cici and her husband Hoop. She's the CFO of the Candied Apple Café," Iona said. "They have a new baby and they are throwing a family-friendly party. And I … well I don't want to overstep but I think you and Sofia would both enjoy it."

Sofia had really enjoyed the party at Jeff's. He remembered how she'd started singing carols. Maybe this party would be good for her. And he admitted he wanted to see Iona again. "What time?"

"Seven. But you could come later if that is better," she said. "I'll text you the address when we get off the phone." She paused. "Thank you, Mads."

"No, thank you. Usually we don't do much for the holidays," he said.

"When did your wife get sick? I think Sofia said she was two," Iona suddenly asked without thinking.

Mads leaned his head back against the pillows and looked up at the ceiling. "That's right. And Gill had chemo and would go into remission for a few months before it came back and we'd

59

go through the entire round of treatments, praying, hoping, then remission again. Most Christmases were spent at home to avoid Gill getting sick from other people, since chemo kills the immune system."

"That had to have been hard for you," Iona said carefully. There was a note of empathy in her voice.

It had been hard on him, but he and Gill had made a commitment to each other when they'd both been young and happy and very much in love. "You know what was the most difficult part? Watching Sofia try to cope with it. The last year when the doctors said they'd done all they could …" he broke off, hearing his own voice crack. What was he going to do? Tell her that Sofia, who thought he could do anything, that he was some sort of superman, had asked him to stop it. To fix Mommy.

"Oh, Mads. I can't even imagine what that's like," Iona said. "Sofia is pretty resilient and I think you are doing a great job with her."

He wiped his eyes with his thumbs. Then took a deep breath. "I hope so. It's hard to judge that since I'm always right in the mix with her. She's so sassy sometimes … I'm not sure that's good."

"It's perfect," Iona said. "In fact, today while she was at the shop picking out her chocolates, she kind of inspired us."

"She did?"

"Yes. And if you think she'd like to be part of the campaign I'd love to use her in it. We are designing small truffle boxes that are 'naughty and nice'. The 'naughty' truffles will have a hint of heat to them."

Mads loved the idea. Sofia would probably be over the moon when she learned about the campaign. "I'll talk with her and let you know if she wants to be a part of the campaign, but just as a consumer I think it's a fantastic idea."

"Thanks. I'm always trying to keep us one step ahead of the competition and to showcase Hayley's candy-making skills."

"That's part of why we want you to be a partner in the Loughman Group. Have you thought any more about our proposal?"

"We've been busy, but tomorrow I'm going to discuss your proposal with my partners. I think we should have an answer for you by next week."

"Good. I think we would make a good partnership," he said, fishing for an indication of which way she was leaning. She was savvy too, so he supposed she'd catch on, but she might just say something that would give away her position a little.

"Good night, Mads," she said.

"See you Friday."

He stopped to check on his daughter again and then went into his bedroom. It was still hard every night when he walked in and didn't see Gill's lamp on or her sitting in bed reading on her iPad. But tonight, when he glanced at the bed in his mind's eye, he didn't see Gill. He saw Iona.

That scared him and made him realize that he couldn't do this. He wasn't ready for a woman like Iona in his life.

***

Iona got the text from her friends to meet at Sant Ambrose instead of the office and she took her time getting ready before going to join them. She had a little extra time because the coffee shop was closer to her apartment than the Candied Apple Café. But when she got downstairs she saw her brother waiting in the lobby.

"Good morning, sister," Theo said, straightening from the wall and coming over to her.

A light dusting of snow on his dark, black hair and the shoulders of his camel-colored coat indicated he hadn't been waiting long.

"Theo, hey," she said. "What are you doing here? Is Mom okay?"

"She's fine," he said. "We were worried about you because you

61

haven't been in our group chat lately. I volunteered to check on you. You can ignore the phone and a text, but in person, we both know I can run faster."

She shook her head. "That's only because I'm in heels. I've been busy. The Candied Apple Café Christmas is taking up a lot of my time. I have to keep us in the public's eye so consumers keep coming in."

"I'm going to say something and if you want to punch me for it, so be it," Theo began. "You don't have to keep trying to prove to us that you are as good at business as dad is."

"I'm not …"

"Don't bother. We both know it's true," he said. "The thing about Dad was he never saw either of us as we truly were. He wanted to believe I was his golden child and that you were Mom's mini-me. He never realized the opposite was true. You have surpassed his drive and determination in business, Io. You can stop. You beat him."

She shook her head. She didn't know how to stop. She only knew the next goal, the next campaign, the next quarter's promotions. "I know you're right."

"Of course I am. It's me," Theo said, without a hint of modesty. "I also know you aren't going to just stop. But if you could find something to do that wasn't business … that would ease the worry Mom and I feel about you."

"I'll try."

"That's all I ask," he said.

He hugged her, holding her tightly and suddenly that knot deep inside her loosened. She knew she had to deal with this thing with her dad, but he was gone and she had been struggling to figure it out.

Tears burned her eyes but she blinked until they were gone and stepped back. "I am heading to a meeting at Sant Ambrose. Want to walk with me and grab a drink until the girls get there."

"You know it," he said. "I had to leave the apartment early to catch you, which meant no coffee in bed."

She shook her head as they left the lobby of the building and noticed it was empty except for the doorman. She took Theo's hand and drew him into a corner.

"I'm *so* happy you found love with Nico," she admitted.

"Me too. It was unexpected. Thanks for being so cool about it," Theo said.

"Well, there was more passion when Nico looked at you than when he kissed me, so I figured I should nudge him toward you," Iona said. "Are you bringing him to the *Nutcracker* next week?"

"I am. What about you?"

"Maybe," she said, knowing Sofia would love the children's event. But she was kind of trying to figure out Mads. He'd kissed her and then played it all cool … what exactly was going on with him?

"Maybe?"

"That's it for now. I'll let you know if it changes."

"Fair enough. I have some news," he said.

She didn't correct her brother that she and Mads were seeing each other. Technically, they *were* seeing each other.

"What's your news?"

"Nico asked me to marry him," Theo said, bursting with joy.

"That's wonderful. I better be the best woman."

"I wouldn't have anyone else!"

He hugged her and then walked with her to Sant Ambrose and she thought she did a great job of acting like her old self. She knew she was going to have keep faking it until she made it. And she'd do it. She had always been there for Theo and she wasn't going to let him down now.

She hugged him and said goodbye to him outside the small coffee shop, then went inside to find her friends waiting at the back of the restaurant.

"Hey you. How was your night?" Cici asked.

"Not bad," Iona said, remembering her late-night chat with Mads.

"Mine was filled with a vision of sugar plums," Hayley said with a wink. "I think I've got an idea for the second 'naughty' truffle. I love this idea."

"Me too. And I was thinking maybe we could use Sofia in the print ad in the shop. Having a little girl do the 'naughty and nice' thing will keep it innocent. I've spoken to her father."

"When did you have time to do that?" Hayley asked.

"Last night," Iona said. "Also, I'm bringing them with me to your party on Friday, Cici."

Cici and Hayley looked at each other and then back at her. "Really?"

"Yes," Iona said and then quickly changed the subject to the deal that the Loughman Group were offering them. She tried to keep her mind on business but she couldn't help it from drifting to Mads.

**

Mads sat down at his desk just after four p.m. for the first time since he'd arrived at the Common that morning. He'd had a restless night of sleep remembering the one kiss he'd shared with Iona and finally admitting that he wanted more. It had been a long day and when he saw the stack of Christmas cards on his desk waiting for him to sign, he shoved them to the side. He wasn't interested in sending corporate holiday greetings at this moment.

He was in a bad mood.

He'd barely had time to see Sofia at breakfast that morning before he'd had to run to the office and realizing that the duty manager was incompetent hadn't helped the day. But the truth was, he knew it was guilt influencing him. He didn't like thinking about moving on from Gill in any way.

He knew it was "healthy" but really that didn't do a thing to make him feel better. He went to the little fridge in his office and opened it to see it was stocked with mineral and sparkling water and a fruit juice that he kept for Sofia's office visits. But he wanted something stronger.

He couldn't drink at work.

He drew the line at that. He'd prided himself on always keeping his head and not turning to any crutches during Gill's illness or death. And he wasn't going to start now.

Without thinking, he dialed Iona's number and she answered on the third ring.

"It's Mads," he said by way of greeting.

"Hey. We still haven't made a decision about the Loughman group."

"Fair enough. I was calling to see if you'd like to join Sofia and me for dinner instead?"

"I'd love to," she said, surprised by his invitation.

He gave her their apartment number and she started laughing. "What?"

"You're only five doors down from me," she said.

It was funny to think she'd been living so close to him but they'd never met until he tried to do business with her.

He and Gill had been excited to move into their home in Brooklyn when they'd gotten married, and after she'd died he'd been unable to stay there any longer. He and Sofia had picked out the apartment where they lived now because it was close to her school.

"What time should I come over?" Iona asked.

Just like that, he was reminded again of how life moved on. She was still making plans for tonight while he was mired in the past. He had to do this. For Sofia. He had to figure out life without Gill.

"Six. Jessie is off tonight so we'll be making spaghetti," he said.

"Yum. My favorite. Can I bring something?" she asked.

"Nah. Jessie already took care of the shopping," he said. "See you later."

He hung up, closing the refrigerator, which he hadn't realized he'd left open. He went back to his desk, pulling the stack of Christmas cards to him. The cards were custom made, a hand-drawn image of the Common decked out for Christmas while snow fell. He remembered approving the design back in July. He opened the first card and sprawled his signature. He made short work of the cards and then stacked them in the outbox for Lexi to take care of.

Last year he'd completely forgotten about sending personal cards to friends and family and he wondered if he should send something this year. But he had no idea where to start. It was late in the season to be thinking of this.

He leaned forward and put his forehead in his hands. *Christmas.* How was he going to do this? He'd never been that good at hiding his emotions. He had a quick temper and no real poker face to speak of so everyone usually knew what he felt. But being a father had changed that. Had forced him to learn how to curb his reactions. But this … he realized that he'd been doing okay until this month.

The last month that Gill had been alive. After this she'd be gone a year. There would be no more first holidays without her. He wasn't sure how he felt about that.

He had almost managed to dull the ache he'd felt when he thought of her death but it was back in full force. A stabbing pain in his heart — not literally — but still there. And he'd invited another woman for spaghetti night. He knew he shouldn't have, but tonight he needed the distraction.

He needed to have something to smile about and no matter what else he felt about Iona, she made him laugh.

"You look like you're ready for a fight."

He glanced up to his see his younger brother Piers standing in the doorway. "Is that why you're here?"

"It wasn't my original intention but I'm always happy to oblige."

Mads smiled. He got up and went around his desk to hug his brother. "I've got a meeting with the Food Network to possibly use the Los Angeles location for a new show they are doing. It wrapped up early so I thought I'd check in on you."

"I'm glad you did," Mads said. "We've got the usual odd crap going on at the hotel. A leak over the merchandise shop."

"I saw the emails about it. Did you get it sorted?" Piers asked.

"Pretty much," he said. "Are you free for dinner?"

"If it means seeing my favorite niece, then yes," Piers said.

"She's your only one," Mads reminded him. Having his brother at dinner would mean it wasn't a date with Iona. There would be no chance of anything untoward. Which didn't explain why he wanted to punch something.

"And my favorite."

Chapter 7

Iona walked the short distance down the hall to Mads and Sofia's apartment, carrying a stuffed moose that wore a tee-shirt that proclaimed "Christmas is for Miracles", and a bottle of Glenlivet she'd been gifted from a client. She didn't drink scotch, but her gut said that Mads probably did. She knocked on the door; it was opened by Sofia and a man that Iona hadn't met.

"Hey, Iona. We raced to the door and I won!" Sofia said. She was in her stockinged feet and jeans and a tee-shirt that had some Disney princesses on it.

"I'm not surprised, you're very fast," Iona said.

"I am," Sofia agreed.

"This is for you," Iona said, handing her the moose.

She took it from Iona and then hugged it to her chest. "Thank you."

"You're welcome."

"Come in," the man said, holding out his hand. "I'm Piers: Mads' younger and some say better-looking brother."

Iona took Piers' hand and shook it, smiling at him. Now that he'd said they were brothers it was easy to see the resemblance. But while Mads seemed too serious, Piers had an easy smile and open charm that Mads didn't. She guessed that the strain of his wife's illness had contributed to that.

"I'll have to reserve judgment on the last bit until I see you side by side."

"Iona."

"Yes?" She glanced down at Sofia.

"Obviously Papa is better-looking. Uncle Piers is just being silly," Sofia said. "Everyone knows my papa is the best."

"Everyone does know that, Sof," Piers said. "Let's move this party into the kitchen so we can help finish making dinner."

Iona followed Sofia down the hall, aware that Piers was behind her. She stepped into the kitchen and noticed that Mads was working at the stove, stirring a tomato sauce. He glanced over his shoulder as they entered and smiled at her.

She raised her eyebrows at him. "Hi. This is for you."

She set the scotch on the counter, out of the way.

"Thanks. Who won the race?"

"Me," Sofia said.

"Congrats," he said to his daughter.

"Iona gave me this moose," Sofia said, holding it up toward Mads. "Want to come to my room while I introduce him to my other stuffies?"

"Unless you need my help?" she asked Mads.

"Nah, Piers is on the garlic bread and Sof already made the salad."

"Okay, then take me to your room," Iona said to Sofia.

The little girl skipped out of the kitchen past her uncle, who stood in the doorway, with Iona following her down the hall past a large living room lined with bookcases on one wall and an entertainment center on another one. She stopped at the third door and opened it up.

"This is my room," she said, stepping inside. It had a single bed in the center of the large room. The bed had a canopy and was loaded with pillows and stuffed animals and dolls. The comforter was a pretty dark-pink colored one. There was a white dust ruffle around the bottom of the bed. And the wall was decorated with princesses and castles. Knights in armor battled against dragons.

It was a fanciful room for a girl who didn't believe in Santa. "You like knights and princesses?"

"Yes. My mom used to read the stories to me when she was sick. I'd sit in her bed with her."

"No wonder you love them," Iona said. "My mom used to read to me when I was your age."

"Did you have a favorite book?"

"I liked *The Secret Three*," Iona said. "It's about three friends who share a secret at the beach. What's your favorite?"

"*Good Night, Good Knight*," she said. "Want to see it?"

"Sure," Iona said, moving into the room and sitting down on the love seat near the window. Sofia kept the moose with her as she went to her bookcase and brought back the book. The first thing Iona noticed was that someone had tampered with the cover. Where the Knight had clearly been a boy before it was now a girl with a pink tutu and long black braids.

"Mommy and I worked to make the book more for me," Sofia said.

She found herself feeling a little emotional thinking of Sofia's mother, knowing she was going to die and trying to give her daughter as much as she could before her time was up. Hayley's mother had also died when Hayley was eighteen and had left her a bunch of letters to open each year on her birthday. Iona felt so lucky to still have her own mom.

"This is perfect. The knight looks just like you," Iona said.

"Yes. The dragon looks like Mommy," Sofia said, climbing up on the love seat next to Iona and opening the book. Sofia read the entire book to her and it was a cute story, but having been doctored by Sofia and her mother it was even more special. When she finished reading it, Sofia left the book on the love seat.

"Do you want to meet all my stuffies?"

"Sure."

She led Iona to the bed and slowly went through each of the stuffed animals and plush dolls on the bed. Iona knew there was no way she was going to remember any of the names of them. Sofia set the moose, which she'd named Iona, in the middle and that was when Iona noticed the teddy bear sitting in the corner facing the wall.

"What's going on over there?"

"That's Mr. Bees and he's been very bad," Sofia said.

"What'd he do?"

"Left all the toys out yesterday. I had to clean them up and Jessie wasn't too happy about it," Sofia said.

"Wow. That is naughty," Iona said.

"I know. I gave him a talking to and then a time out," Sofia said. "He can probably go back up on the bed now."

She went to get him and told him she still loved him but he needed to follow the rules, which made Iona smile, thinking that this was probably something that Sofia had experienced when she misbehaved.

***

Mads didn't know what he'd expected but the evening had turned out to be a lot of fun. Sofia was full of beans and after dinner she was running around with a lot of energy. Mads could feel the stress of the day coming back as he had to repeatedly tell her to settle down as she jumped from the sofa to the love seat, and he knew he was about to lose it and stood up.

"Sofia."

She dropped down on the cushion, her face turning red. "Sorry, Papa."

"That's okay," he said. "Don't do that again. We don't jump on furniture."

"Yes, sir," Sofia said.

"I should probably head out," Iona said. "Mads, I wanted to speak to you about the dinner party on Friday."

"Why don't you walk her home?" Piers suggested. "I'll supervise this one getting ready for bed and let her read me a story."

It all sounded so reasonable. There was no way he could say no, that he didn't want to be alone with Iona right now. The night had been fun, the kind of evening that they had needed. He and Sofia. He got it. Understood why she had been jumping on the furniture. Tonight, there was no gap in their family. Tonight had felt almost like a normal evening.

And later he might feel guilty, but right now he really just wished he could enjoy it.

"Sounds good," Mads said. He kissed Sofia on the top of her head and then followed Iona to the door.

She wore a pair of skinny jeans and a tunic thermal top that ended at the tops of her thighs and a pair of ankle boots that gave her another inch of height. But she still only came to his shoulder. She seemed the right height to fit into his arms perfectly. He remembered that one brief brush of their lips and knew that he wanted more.

He needed something that he'd been denying himself for a long time. And it wasn't sex. It was this kind of quiet intimacy that he felt as they walked down the hall together. She was talking quietly about the event on Friday but he wasn't paying attention at all.

"So, this is kind of awkward," she said. "But, umm, do you want to come in?"

"Why is that awkward?" he asked.

"I meant my brother. I have something to tell you," she said. "Didn't you hear me?"

He shook his head. "Sorry, Iona, I wasn't paying attention. Yes, I'll come in."

She nodded and he followed her into her place. It was a similar layout to his apartment but was decorated with brighter colors.

She led the way into the kitchen breakfast nook and flipped on the light.

"Do you want something to drink?"

"Am I going to need it?" he asked.

Her lips twitched in a half smile. "No. I don't think so."

"Then I'm good," he said, pulling out one of the ladder- back chairs at her table and sitting down. She walked around the table and sat across from him. The light from the pendulum lamp fell on her head, making him notice that her red hair had some gold highlights in it.

"So … I wanted to invite you and Sofia to join me at the New York City Ballet's *Nutcracker* event. We've always gone and my family has a table."

"I have already booked a table. Sofia wanted to go. Could you join us instead?" he asked.

"Let me talk to my mom and make sure she won't be upset."

"Fair enough," he said. "I think Sofia would love to have you there. She's really taken to you."

"Tonight, she showed me the book she and her mommy made. It was so sweet and special," Iona said.

Mads loved that storybook but had a hard time when Sofia suggested they read it together. Some days he was okay, but he'd found grief wasn't always predictable and other times it hit him hard.

But not tonight. The memories of Gill were fond and soft and somehow he thought it might be down to Iona.

"This is the last month of firsts without Gill and then … I don't know what will happen," he said. "I promised her I'd keep moving forward, but it's hard."

Iona reached over and took his hand gently. "You're not alone. I think it's safe to say that you and I are becoming friends."

"Maybe," he said. But deep inside he knew he wanted something more than just a friendship with her. He wanted her to show him a way out of the darkness and into the new year. But he wasn't sure that was something he could actually do.

"Maybe?"

"I might want to be more than friends, though," he admitted.

***

The day had to be one of her oddest in recent memory. But it had ended well. She'd enjoyed dinner with Mads. His family dynamic was different than hers. Mads and Piers were both strong personalities but they were also close, or at least seemed to be. It sharpened her own guilt about the situation with her brother.

She knew it was her own fault and after talking to her friends earlier and now talking to Mads, it helped her to deal with it. When she expressed her feelings out loud she felt silly. And keeping them inside had made her feel more and more embarrassed.

Mads' dark eyes were filled with concern and maybe she was projecting but it also seemed to her that he watched her mouth more often than not.

She wanted to know what it would be like to kiss him properly. That brief brush of lips at Rockefeller Center had done nothing to assuage her curiosity; his kiss in front of the building had whetted her appetite for more. His hands were big in hers and she knew that no matter how much he might want to kiss her, there was still that world of firsts he'd mentioned. He was a widower and a part of him was still dealing with how to live without his wife. The other part was struggling with raising Sofia on his own.

That little girl who believed in princesses and knights should believe in Santa. She should still have that innocence that Iona knew she'd lost when her mom had died. And Iona knew she couldn't bring her mom back but she hoped she could help to make this holiday a happy one for them both.

Mads shifted in his chair, pulling his hands from hers, rubbing his thumb over her knuckles and sending a shot of awareness through her. She had the feeling he wanted more than friendship too.

"You're awfully quiet," he said.

She shrugged. No way was she telling him that she wanted to know what it would be like to feel his lips against hers again. But then her own lips felt dry and she licked them, shifting in the chair.

He arched one eyebrow at her.

"I'm guessing you're distracted by the same thing I was in the hallway earlier."

She doubted it. He'd probably been thinking about his daughter … she hadn't realized until this moment what a hit to the ego losing Theo had been to her. She hadn't dated anyone since August, when and he and Nico had gotten together.

Usually she immediately would have moved onto another man but she had felt the need to retreat into herself instead.

"What distracted you?"

"You," he said. "I was wondering what it would be like to really kiss you again."

She nibbled at her lower lip. "I don't know if that's a good idea."

He didn't say anything else. It was clear to her from what she knew of him that Mads was more comfortable with action.

Her heart started to pound in her chest. He got up and came around the table. He stopped and leaned against it, turning so he was facing her. No way was she walking away from him now. She'd been thinking about that snowy kiss he'd given her for days and she wanted more.

She stood up and he put his hand on her waist and his other hand on her upper arm. Lightly holding her, not moving closer to her. But just holding her lightly and letting her decide what happened next. She shifted closer to him, putting both hands on his waist and holding onto him like he was her anchor.

He tipped his head to the side and she went up on her tiptoes and their lips met. That electric tingle went through her again. Then he opened his mouth over hers, deepening the kiss as he pulled her into his arms.

She wrapped hers around him as she gave herself up to the moment and the passion that he'd been stirring inside of her since the moment they met. She'd fooled herself into thinking that she only wanted him as a friend when the reality was she wanted so much more.

Chapter 8

Mads hadn't been able to resist Iona anymore. He just wanted to forget for a few hours, in her arms. He had been carrying around that mantle of guilt for too long. He had no idea if this would amount to more than an affair, but he couldn't just walk away.

Not tonight.

He'd been right about her fitting perfectly in his arms. Her lips moved under his, returning the kiss, and he had to admit it felt good to be held by a woman again. He let himself just enjoy the feel of her breasts against his chest and the notch at the top of her thighs created a perfect place for his erection. He thrust his hips forward against her and felt an answering thrust from her in return. He caressed her back as his tongue edged into her mouth. She tasted of the coffee they'd drunk after dinner and she smelled like peppermint and pine. Like Christmas. Like all the things that he kept proclaiming to be annoyed by.

But she also felt so right that he knew that was a lie.

He ran his hand down her back, cupping her butt and drawing her more fully into the curve of his body as she rocked against him. Her hands tightening on his waist, drawing him even closer to her. He canted his hips forward again, moving one leg between hers as he grabbed her backside and pulled her closer to him. He tilted his head and angled his mouth for a deeper kiss. His pulse pounded loudly in his ears, drowning out the last vestiges of doubt he had, keeping him from thinking too hard about this moment.

God, she tasted good.

He knew he should pull back and take this slow but he couldn't. He swept his hands to her waist and then skimmed it over the side of her breast as she lifted one of her arms and wrapped it around his shoulder.

She seemed to be forgetting herself as well. It was as if this was exactly what they both needed. Something to make them forget the reality they were both dealing with. Sex was the best way to forget.

He knew that. But this was more than sex.

Damn.

He had to shut down his mind but he couldn't. This was another first; kissing a woman he cared about. It wasn't a one-night stand where he'd walk away from her and never see her again.

Hell, she lived in his building.

She pulled back from him and he looked at her.

"You're distracted by something else now," she said. "I'm guessing this isn't what you want anymore."

Crap.

"No, that's not it," he said. But really, what woman wanted to hear the truth? That he wasn't sure he could kiss her and remain cold inside. And that he'd started to take a certain comfort from the coldness because it kept him from feeling and from the pain that had been too much for him for too long.

But he'd started to thaw. And that was what bothered him. He wasn't ready to rejoin the land of the living. It was one thing for him to kiss a woman he'd walk away from but this was something more. Something he hadn't anticipated.

"Really?" she arched her eyebrow at him. "I'm not dumb. I get it. You have been trying to deal with the fact that Gill is gone and haven't moved on yet. And now I'm here, saying let's be friends …"

"That's partially it," he admitted. "But the truth is, Iona, you keep surprising me. I can't help that I'm a man torn in two by the circumstances of his life."

"I know that," she said quietly. "I get it. I'm just not sure I can handle it right now. Any other time I'd be able to smile and kiss you and take you to my bed so we could have some fun, but I like you. I like your daughter and she seems to need me as a friend too. So we really can't just casually sleep together, Mads."

Mads ran his hand through his hair. He knew all of that. He shouldn't have kissed her but her lips had been too tempting. Her mouth always drew his attention whenever he was with her and kissing her was something he'd thought about even though he hadn't wanted to. He knew then that he had to decide if he was going to give in to his desire for her and if that was the case, he had to commit. No more of this …

"I think it's time you left," she said. "I'm just not able to do this. Not tonight. The next time I see you — Friday for Cici's party — I'll be back to my old self."

She walked away from him and he watched as she leaned against the kitchen counter, crossing her legs at the ankles and wrapping her arms around her chest. She was hurting and he'd just wounded her a little more. He'd wanted to somehow make things better for them both and had failed.

Now he felt like an ass.

Probably he was an ass.

He swallowed hard and took a step closer to her and she gave him a hard look that warned him she wasn't in the mood to be placated and he understood that. He shouldn't have started something he couldn't finish but honestly until he'd taken her in his arms he hadn't realized how much Iona had come to mean to him.

"Sorry. You're just the first woman I've cared about whom I've kissed since Gill. And it's harder than I thought it would be."

She shook her head sadly at him. "Don't say things you don't mean."

"I never do," he said.

***

Iona wanted to believe him, which was a clear indication to her that she was in over her head. "You can't mean that."

"Why can't I?" he asked.

What was she going to say? That she wasn't the right woman for him. She'd learned one thing from Theo and Nico and that was what the heart wanted, it wanted. She couldn't control who she fell for any more than anyone else could.

And falling for Mads had dumb written all over it. He was a man who was coming back into the land of the living, not a man who she should be thinking about falling for.

But she couldn't help it. She liked him, as she'd observed earlier when she'd given in to her desire to kiss him. He liked her, but a big part of her knew that it couldn't be the same. She was never going to be more than his transition person.

"I'm not sure either of us is in a position to deal with this."

He smiled at her and his entire face looked so much younger. Until that moment she never had noticed that he rarely smiled and he always had a look of someone who was doing his best to survive each day.

Her heart melted a little bit and though she knew that she was a big girl and way too old to believe in wishes whispered on a cold December night, her heart made one. It wanted Mads to be hers and to be real.

"Let's just be honest with each other. No promises or commitments," he said.

That appealed more than she wanted to admit, so she nodded and then smiled over at him. "And if I change my mind?"

"Just let me know. If I'm in the same spot, we'll do whatever it is," he said. He rubbed the back of his neck. "It's been hard for me to differentiate between what's real and what's me just trying to survive, but there is something about you, Iona, that hasn't left my mind from the moment we met."

Because she wanted what he was saying to be true she had to lighten the moment or at least try to. They were getting too real. Too serious and she still wasn't sure she could trust him or herself. "Never under-estimate the power of a short skirt and a pair of tights."

"I'm not denying that you have killer legs and could make a grown man believe in Santa Claus again, but there is more to it than that."

He just kept saying the right things and she was having a hard time remembering to take things slow. To just go with it, as he'd suggested. To be fair, she'd never been a "just go with it" person, which was probably a big part of her dating problems.

"Am I making you think differently about the season?" she asked, letting her arms fall to her side and standing up straighter. It was time to get him out of her apartment before she lost the argument with herself that said she needed to be cautious around him and did something that would feel good but she'd regret in the morning.

"You are," he admitted. "Not that I'm ever going to believe that miracles are possible, I just can't go there again. But you are making things different for me and for Sofia."

"She's such a sweet child," Iona said. "How did the chocolates go over at school?"

"Pretty well. The teacher thought it was a nice gesture and then tonight Remy called to say thank you and to apologize for saying she was naughty. She was happy with that. I think things

81

are going to be okay now."

"I'm glad to hear it," Iona said.

"Is this your way of telling me it's time to go home?" he asked.

"I think so. Today ... well it's been a long day and I'm ready to crash," she admitted. "I recorded *A Charlie Brown Christmas* and I think I need to watch that tonight."

"Then I'll leave you to it," he said, walking towards the door and she followed him.

She decided then and there that she was going to give him some space for the next few days. She needed to regain her perspective. She had started out with a plan but that had flown into the wind the first time he'd kissed her and tonight ... well for a few moments she'd thought she'd found something in his arms. But then ...

"Never mind," she said out loud, startled to hear her own voice.

Crap.

"Never mind, what?"

That was one embarrassing habit she wished she could get rid of but whenever she was stressed she often spoke thoughts that she wished she'd kept quiet. "Just trying to still my mind, which is busy making more arguments than I can deal with right now."

"Good luck with that," he said. "I've never found anything that could make me forget, except maybe for those few seconds when I was kissing you."

They'd gotten to her foyer and she leaned back against her front door. "And then your mind went totally crazy. And you started thinking about Gill again."

"I didn't say it was easy," he admitted.

"I don't think it should be. I can tell you two had a deep love and if I were the one in your shoes I think I'd be struggling too."

"Thank you," he said, after a few moments had passed.

"For what?"

"Just understanding," he said. Then he hugged her close and

reached around her to open the door and walked out. She stood there watching him for a moment before she realized what she was doing and closed the door, locking it and then sinking to the floor and staring at the foyer tiles, telling herself she was okay. But something made her feel like she never would be again.

***

Mads cancelled the dinner party with Iona. Sofia wasn't too happy with him and the leak at the hotel had turned out to be a major plumbing issue, which of the three things was the easiest to deal with, so he was focusing there.

His brother had flown back to the West Coast, issuing an invitation for him and Sofia to join him out there for Christmas. And he was seriously thinking about taking him up on it. He wasn't sure why he thought staying in Manhattan would be the right thing to do. But he'd wanted Christmas … hell, he no longer knew. He was sitting in his office supposedly fixing the plumbing issue and trying to reassign guests, some of their highest-profile guests visited during the holidays and he had to balance their regular customer visits with the VIPs who wanted to stay. It was a bit of a nightmare and he'd been in meetings most of the day with everyone on the staff, including maintenance, who had called in extra staff to help facilitate the outside plumbing company they'd had to hire.

Mads had been assured that they would have the problem fixed tonight, which was the excuse he'd given Iona when he'd cancelled. He knew she didn't want to be flying solo at a party that was for families, but after the other night, he had been unable to remember what Gill's kiss tasted like and that had felt like the ultimate betrayal, especially when he'd fallen into a restless sleep and dreamed he was making love to a woman and that woman was Iona.

He wanted her and he'd been hoping, despite the fact that he had already admitted it was more than lust, that he'd still be able to contain his desire for her. That he'd somehow be able to keep her in the friends with benefits zone instead of dreaming about her. Remembering her kiss and the taste of it in a way he wasn't sure he'd ever done with Gill.

He put his head in his hands as his office phone rang. He'd sent Lexi home, so had told her to forward her line to him in case there were issues with the maintenance.

"Mads Eriksson."

"Oh, hello there," Iona said. "I'm sorry to call like this but we have an extra guest at our party and I thought you'd want to know."

"What are you talking about? Why are you being so vague?" he asked.

"That's right. We need to see about getting another child's dish," Iona said.

"Is Sofia at your friend's party?" he asked.

"Yes. I have the young lady right here and she'd like …" Iona said, then seemed to cover the mouthpiece. "What do you want for dinner?"

"Chicken," Sofia said. He could tell by the note in her voice that she was feeling defiant.

"Is she alone?"

"Yes. I don't think we'll need anything else. Do you need the address?" she asked.

"I've got it. I'll be right there."

"Great," Iona said. "I think that's for the best."

She hung up. His cell phone rang. He saw it was Jessie.

"Mads. Oh, my God. I can't find Sofia. I think she's run away. Which makes no sense …"

"I know where she is."

"Thank God. Where is she?" Jessie asked.

"She went to the party we were supposed to attend tonight," Mads said. "How did she get out of the apartment?"

"I was getting changed," Jessie replied. "We went to Central Park to play in the snow and when we got back, I ran a bath for her and went to change. I checked on her ten minutes later and she was gone. I've been searching everywhere. It's so unlike her."

"It *is* unlike her."

"Where is she? Send me the address and I'll go and get her."

"NO, that's okay. I'll get her. I think I need to talk to her. Why don't you take the rest of the night off?" Mads suggested.

"I don't think I can until I see her and know she's okay," Jessie said. "I promised Gill I would keep her safe and raise her like she was my own."

He heard the crack in Jessie's voice. "You're doing great. This is on me. She likes Iona. She was really upset when I told her we couldn't go. I'll text you when we are on our way home."

"Thanks," Jessie said.

Mads went down to check with the maintenance manager who was overseeing the work. He let him know that he had to leave and asked to be kept informed of anything that happened. He also talked to the GM before leaving the Common.

Hamlisch met him up front. "Home, sir?"

"No. We're going to this address," he said, rattling it off.

He got into the back seat as Hamlisch closed the door and a few minutes later they were on their way. He watched the city lights flashing by his window as they drove and he could only think of all the ways he was screwing up. It hadn't even been a year since Gill died and Sofia had run away.

He knew he had to be better than this with her, but, honestly, at this moment he didn't know what else to do. It was hard dealing with his grief. Managing his next steps when he also had to manage Sofia's, and it wasn't like he was making excuses but tonight he felt like he had a million reasons why he couldn't keep doing this.

Hamlisch pulled up in front of the building and Mads asked him to wait for them. He took a minute to compose himself. He knew that going in there in full temper wasn't the right thing to do. But he also knew he couldn't just let her get away with her actions. She was six not sixteen. And what she had done was very dangerous.

Chapter 9

Iona saw the look of anger and panic on Mads' face as he entered Cici's apartment. The party was in full swing with lots of music, conversation, and laughter. He scanned the crowd and she was already walking towards him as their eyes met. She'd wanted to avoid him after that kiss in her apartment, but running away had never been her thing and she'd been surprised when he'd cancelled tonight.

She knew he'd mentioned work and completely understood that a leak in the hotel during one of the busiest seasons was a major emergency but a part of her had felt like he had been playing an avoidance game.

Iona had been surprised when Sofia had shown up. She'd looked defiant and scared as she'd knocked on the door and immediately Iona knew that the little girl had come on her own. Sofia was helping decorate the tree that Cici and Hoop had set up in the corner of the living room.

Hoop had taken to fatherhood and family like a man who'd waited a lifetime to have one of his own.

"Where is she?" Mads asked as they met in the foyer.

"Helping decorate the tree. You look pissed. Do you want to calm down before you talk to her?" Iona suggested.

"No," Mads said. Then shoved his hand through his hair. "I don't think I can. She's all I have left. This isn't acceptable."

"I know. I think she knows that too. She looked scared when she got here. Cici's doorman brought her up after paying for the cab."

"She took a cab without any money?" Mads asked.

Iona could tell he was on the edge of losing it. "Don't think about what could have gone wrong. She's safe now. Come on. She's been playing with baby Holly. She's my friends' daughter. She's barely three months old and Sofia seems enchanted with her."

Iona had been thinking she'd just let Mads and Sofia have their reunion by themselves but she felt the desperation in Mads and knew he was on the edge. She'd heard it in his voice. *She's all I have left.*

No one should feel that way. But Iona understood it. She slipped her hand into Mads and he remained stiff for a second and then squeezed hers. "Thank you."

She nodded. She wasn't truly certain if he was thanking her for the comfort or for keeping his daughter safe until he got here. Or if he just was saying thanks for the friendship.

Again, it came back to that. He needed a friend. And she might want more — okay, definitely wanted more — it was impossible not to look at that thick curly black hair and not want to run her fingers through it or to look at his legs in those incredibly tight jeans and not think about how they felt entangled with hers as they'd kissed.

But she knew she needed to.

Lust wasn't the foundation of anything. Except a night of fun.

They approached the tree and Mads stopped as they got close enough to see Sofia bent over the baby seat that Holly was in. She had turned the seat so that the baby could see the twinkling lights. Sofia was sitting on the floor next to the baby.

"This one is a star. And this is a reindeer. They live in the colder places. Like way colder than it gets here. And they can be used to pull sleighs but they can't fly," Sofia said. "Some people think that they can fly but that's not true."

The baby cooed and Sofia smiled.

Mads moved past Iona and crouched down next to his daughter. "I guess they must pull the sleigh really fast so that to some it feels like flying."

"Papa."

"Sofia."

"This is Holly," Sofia said, not looking up at Mads but still staring at the baby.

"You know we have to talk about this," Mads said.

"I do know. I'm sorry, Papa," she said, turning towards him. "It wasn't Jessie's fault."

"I already figured that out when she called me in a panic," Mads said.

"I'm in big trouble, aren't I?"

"Let's just say that you have definitely earned the naughty label tonight," Mads said.

Iona noticed that he had complete control over his temper and though he'd seemed angry with his daughter, now that he was knelt beside her under the Christmas tree he was completely calm. "Have you been explaining Christmas to Holly?"

"As best I can. There are a lot of grown-ups here and Iona had to go and talk to someone else."

"Sorry, darling," Iona said.

"It's okay. Did you call Papa?"

"I did. As much as I love having you here, I suspected he didn't really know where you were."

"It's okay. I forgive you," Sofia said.

"You forgive her?" Mads asked.

"For telling on me," Sofia said.

"She didn't tell on you. She let us know where you were, Sofia. Jessie and I were worried and no one could find you. If Iona hadn't called me I would have gone to the police."

"Why?"

"They are the only ones who could help find you," Mads continued. "That's what happens when parents can't find their kids."

Sofia's hand dropped away from the baby seat and she threw herself into Mads' arms, knocking him off balance. He caught her and held her close to him. She was saying something that Iona couldn't hear and she knew she should leave the two of them alone to work out everything.

Reaching around Mads and Sofia, she scooped up Holly's baby seat and took her across the room to the kitchen. It was quieter there and she thought she was alone until she noticed Hayley in the corner kissing her fiancé Garrett. She turned her back on them, looking down at Holly, who cooed softly.

Iona had an eye-opening moment as she realized as much as she loved her work with the Candied Apple Café, she wanted this too. *She wasn't her father.* Damn. That had taken her a long time to accept. Theo had been right when he said she was going to have to figure out for herself that success in business wasn't going to satisfy her forever.

Why did it have to happen now? When she was at a party and dealing with being a good friend to a man whose kisses she couldn't forget and who made her want things she had no idea she could handle?

She took Holly down the hall to her room, lifting the baby out of the carrier and held her in her arms. She smelled sweet, like baby powder and lotion. Her little body was encased in a onesie that was red and white-striped and she rested her head on Iona's shoulder as she rocked her back and forth.

It wasn't that hard to figure out that she wanted a family of her own since everyone else she knew had one. The hard part was reconciling the fact that the man she'd fixated on to be a part of it wasn't ready for that.

***

Sofia had apologized and settled down and he looked around for Iona to thank her once again for calling him. But he couldn't find her. She had left them alone to work things out. One of Iona's friends offered him some food and after Sofia admitted she hadn't eaten because she'd been worried about getting in trouble, he accepted the offer and made them both a plate. They found a quiet nook near the dining room to eat.

"I'm glad you were upset when you got here," Mads said. "That tells me you know what you did was wrong."

"I do," Sofia said.

"Why did you do it?"

She shrugged and played with the food on her plate.

"That's not an answer, Sof. It's okay if you don't know why."

She looked up at him, her eyes so big and earnest that his heart took a punch. He had tried his best to protect her from everything, but her mom had been sick for most of her recent memory and was gone. There had only been so much he could do and seeing that look, well, it made him wish he could have done something different.

"I just wanted it to feel like … well not like last year," she admitted. "And parties and stuff are."

He nodded. "I had a real emergency at work tonight so I'm sorry we had to cancel. But perhaps I can see about making other arrangements if it happens again. Running off is never the solution."

"I know that now," Sofia said, then glanced beyond his shoulder. "Hi, Iona. You can join us now. Papa's done yelling at me."

"I didn't yell at you," he said with a gentle smile, looking over at Iona, who stood a few feet away. "Please come and join us."

She walked towards them, bells jingling as she walked but she wasn't wearing her Santa hat. He skimmed his gaze over her body and admitted to himself that he was tired of trying to avoid her. He had missed her and it had only been three days since he saw her. She smiled at Sofia, tipping her head to the side as she spoke and he noticed the jingle bell dangling earrings she wore.

"Is that okay, Papa?"

"I'm sorry, Sof, I wasn't paying attention."

"Can I go and get a cookie from the kitchen?" Sofia asked again, speaking slowly, as if he couldn't understand her.

"Yes, brat," he responded. She smiled and dashed to the kitchen as Iona came and sat down next to him.

"I hope you don't mind but I wanted a moment to talk to you," Iona said.

"I don't mind at all. Thank you again for keeping her safe," he said. There weren't enough words to tell her what that meant to him.

"I'm just glad she came here. How did she know the address?"

"I asked her that earlier and she had seen the address on Jessie's text messages. What's up? You said you wanted to talk to me," he said.

She crossed her legs and glanced over her shoulder first, then leaned in closer to him. She smelled faintly of cinnamon and for a moment he remembered how it had felt to hold her in his arms.

"I wasn't sure if you had canceled because of the other night," she said. "I should apologize, but I liked kissing you and I like you, Mads. And Sofia is just an added bonus to being around you."

"Don't. Don't apologize," he said. He wasn't any closer to really figuring out how to move forward with Iona but tonight, coming here and seeing her, had made it clear that he wasn't going to be able to just walk away. "You have nothing to apologize for. I'm sorry I got weirded out."

"That's fine. I kind of like that you did. It made me realize you're not a casual person when it comes to relationships," she said. She wasn't either. Well, she had been, but not anymore.

92

Something had been changing inside of her since New Year's Day, when Hayley had said she was making a change. She'd sort of set in motion something for Iona too. And now that it was almost the end of the year she knew that she wanted to try something with Mads.

"Good. So, we're still on for the *Nutcracker*, right?" he asked.

"Oh, yes," she said. "Mom was okay with it. Actually, I wondered if you have your own table. Cici and Hayley both overheard me giving up my seat at Mom's table and would love to attend," she said.

"I do. And I think there are seats available. So that should be fine," Mads said. "I'm not being rude but I have to check in with the hotel. The repairs should be done now and I want to make sure we can use the rooms tomorrow."

"Go ahead," Iona said. "I'll find Sofia and meet you in the living room by the tree. Baby Holly loves the lights and I noticed that Cici likes watching her daughter stare at them."

She stood up and he stopped her, standing up and catching her wrist. The action pulled her off balance and she fell into his arms exactly where he wanted her. He lowered his head and kissed her. Closed his eyes and this time there wasn't that painful feeling in his chest. He knew he was kissing Iona and she was the only one he wanted to kiss. She wrapped her arms around him, tipping her head to the side, bells jingling as she deepened the kiss.

***

Singing Christmas carols with her friends, Mads, and Sofia after all the other party guests had left was something … well, really magical. She could see the snow falling beyond the tree through the window that looked over Central Park. Cici and Hoop sat together in a large armchair, Cici cuddling Holly in her arms. Garrett and Hayley were sitting on the floor in front of the tree and Iona and Mads and Sofia were nestled together on the couch.

She knew — truly she did — that this wasn't real. That she and Mads had just become a family without any effort. But a part of her finally admitted it was something she was interested in.

Sofia was starting to get sleepy, curling closer to Mads, resting her head on his chest as Leon Redbone's version of "Winter Wonderland" played in the background. Mads gave her a wry smile. "I think we should go."

She nodded. "I'll come with you."

"I was hoping you'd say that."

She glanced over to see that Hayley was watching her with one eyebrow raised. Her friends had been cool about not saying anything about Sofia arriving by herself or Mads kissing her in the kitchen hallway. But she had the feeling tomorrow at work they were going to want all the details.

She just smiled at Hayley, who winked at her. "We're going to head out. Thanks for a wonderful party."

"You're welcome," Hoop said as he shifted Cici and baby Holly to the chair and stood up. "I'll see them out."

"Thanks."

Iona went over and gave Cici a hug and kissed the sleeping baby on the head before waving bye to Hayley and Garrett. Mads followed her, carrying his daughter, who'd fallen asleep. Iona gathered their coats from Hoop.

"My phone is in my pocket," Mads said. "Will you text Hamlisch we're ready to go?"

She blushed as Hoop watched her reach her hand into Mads' back pocket to retrieve his phone. She tried to be nonchalant but the gesture felt intimate. Not something acquaintances would do. She took out his phone and handed it to him since it was password-protected. She turned to hug Hoop as Mads texted his driver.

He reached around her to open the door for Mads. "See you

on Saturday."

"Can't believe I'm going to the ballet," Hoop said. "But I think it should be fun."

"You'll love it," Iona said.

He nodded and they left the apartment. Iona hit the button for the down elevator and as they waited Mads looked over at her. There was an intensity in his gaze that she hadn't noticed in him before.

"What?"

"I was just thinking about something Sofia had said earlier."

"What was it?" Iona asked, tucking a strand of Sofia's hair behind her ear.

"That she wanted this year to feel different. Gill was sick for three years before she died. Sofia never knew a Christmas that didn't involve nurses or hospitals."

Iona put her arms around them both and hugged them. She wanted them to be hers. She held them tightly because she wanted to keep them close forever. "We're going to make this one special for her."

"I hope it's good for you too," he said.

"Me too," she admitted, as the elevator doors opened. She caught a glimpse of the three of them walking through the lobby in the mirrored wall behind the reception desk. They looked like a family. Like the one she'd kept tucked away in the back of her mind from the moment that her mom had mentioned a match-maker. Finding her a husband because it was time for her to have a family of her own.

Her own.

But that had been her mom's agenda, trying to force her to not work so hard, not be like her dad. This was different. She hadn't been looking for Mads or Sofia when they'd come into her life.

"You okay?" Mads asked.

She realized she'd stopped walking and was staring at her own reflection in the mirror. She nodded because she knew she couldn't tell him what was on her mind. That at this moment she finally got that she hadn't been okay in a really long time. She'd used the Candied Apple as her surrogate family. She'd made that little place into the only thing that mattered in her life because there she was safe. She could pour all of her hopes and dreams into the shop and it would never let her down.

Never break her heart or let her glimpse something she longed to call her own, only to take it away from her.

And she knew … really, she did, that she'd been pretending for too long that the Candied Apple Café would be enough to fill the emptiness left by never getting the approval she needed from her father.

She wanted this Christmas wish that she'd been silently whispering for longer than she could remember to come true. She wanted Christmas morning to be special and not because she'd ordered lots of things she wanted and had them wrapped and delivered and put under her tree. But this year she wanted to have something she couldn't buy. Something that had always been out of her reach and that reflection in the mirror made her hope that this time she could get it.

That Mads and Sofia could be hers, not just on Christmas morning but for all the Christmases to come.

Chapter 10

Sofia slept through the drive back to their building and Iona was quiet. When they got there, she didn't say a word in the elevator and waved goodbye when they got to her door.

He realized that something had changed tonight. He'd realized that work, which had been his salvation when Gill had died, had turned into a crutch. The Duty Manager was more than capable of handling the supervision of the repair and rehousing of guests, but Mads had needed to be there because he hadn't wanted to be home at the holidays too much.

But Sofia needed more. And something told him Iona — his fellow workaholic — did too.

Jessie was waiting for them when they walked in. "I was ready to scold her but she looks so sweet sleeping."

"I already let her know how worried we were. She's going to apologize in the morning."

"Want me to get her settled?" Jessie asked.

"No, I'll do it," Mads said. He carefully got his sleeping daughter into her pajamas and then turned on her nightlight and let himself out of the room.

Jessie was waiting. "I think I'm going to sit on the love seat and watch her for a few moments."

"Okay." He guessed Jessie wanted to make sure her charge was really safe. "Jess, do you mind if I go out for a little while?"

"I don't."

"Text me if you need me," Mads said. He took a bottle of Bailey's that a client had gifted him and walked down the hall to Iona's apartment.

It was late, almost midnight, so he wasn't sure she'd let him in or even if she was still awake, but he had to try.

Tonight, when he'd sat on the couch with her and Sofia, he'd felt something shift. That part that he had carefully kept frozen since Gill's illness was starting to thaw.

And he was tired of fighting his own instincts out of guilt. Out of obligation. He had loved Gill but he knew that he was doing their love a disservice by never letting anyone in his heart again. Not that he was ready to fall in love again, but he was tired of being alone.

He knew if he knocked on her door, he couldn't freak out the way he had the other night when he'd kissed her. He had to be committed to this.

He stared at her front door. The jolly-looking wreath on it. He raised his hand to knock and then let it fall to his side. He wanted to be one hundred percent sure, but he never had been of anything. Not of Gill, not of running the Common. He'd always followed his gut and it had seldom let him down. He hoped that with Iona he would be right as well.

He lifted his hand and knocked. It was firm and in his mind, it was louder than he knew it actually was. He heard it echoing through those empty parts of his soul. He held his breath as he heard the click of the deadbolt and then the door swung open.

"Mads."

She'd changed out of her party wear since he'd left her. She had on a pair of red and white-striped pajama pants and a thermal red shirt. Her hair was up in ponytail and she'd taken off her make-up.

"Can I come in?" he asked.

"Sure," she said, stepping back to let him enter.

He stepped over the threshold and he'd hoped, really hoped, that his nerves would have calmed down, but they didn't. Everything masculine in him was on high alert. He wanted her. He wanted her in his arms, remembered the way she'd felt pressed against him until it was all he thought about. And not just at night either. He'd thought about it in the elevator on his way to work. Imagined taking her in his arms, her mouth under his, her limbs tangled with his. He was tired of being frozen and afraid to let anyone in.

Didn't he want more than this bland friendship they were both trying to pretend was enough? He should have just walked away. It would never be. Not for him and, he suspected, not for her either.

He entered her hallway and noticed that she'd added more things to the hallway table. It was a little village with houses nestled on a white table runner and a lighted ceramic tree in the center of the ring of homes. There was a sleigh nestled on top of the roof of one of the houses and Santa stood near the chimney.

There was lighted garland around the table and he noticed the smell of cinnamon that he was starting to associate with her was stronger here.

"I see you brought Baileys."

"I did. Thought we could both use a drink," he said. "It's been a long week for me."

"Me too. We are running with the 'naughty and nice' truffles. I had the boxes designed with our Candied Apple Café font. We are going to do a big push, starting tomorrow, with them," she said. "But you probably didn't come here to talk about what's on my plate at work. Follow me."

She turned and went down the hall. He noticed that the pajama pants she wore clung to the curve of her backside and emphasized her long legs. The kitchen had a tiled floor and she'd left the light over the stove on, which created an intimate setting as he followed her in.

There was a butcher-block-topped island in the middle of the kitchen area and in the corner was a padded bench with a table in front of it and two chairs on the opposite side. She hit a switch, flipping on the overhead lights. He noticed that she was holding herself back. Normally, her smile was easier and he wondered if this was his gift to her. Stealing her joy of the season while she gave him back his.

He hoped not. She'd really shown him what the holidays could be like without trips to the hospital and midnight calls to the doctor. He had forgotten, he realized.

But the truth was he could no longer remember the man he'd been before Gill had gotten sick. Maybe that was who he was.

"Should I leave?" he asked.

"No," she said. "Let me get us some glasses and ice before we get into that."

She opened one of the top cabinets and took out two whiskey glasses. She put two cubes of ice in each one and brought them to the counter, where he'd been standing. He opened the bottle and poured a generous amount in each one.

She lifted her glass to his. "To drinking at midnight."

He stared at the creamy liquor in the glass. Gill hadn't been much of a drinker, of course, and after the bouts of cancer, chemo, and remission she'd become a ghost of her former self. He remembered … that towards the end he'd felt she was hanging on just because of him.

"Is there a reason why we are?" he asked.

"You brought it," she said. "Is there one for you?"

He leaned forward on the counter, resting his elbows on it. "Maybe," he said, but he wasn't about to unload on her. He needed to man up. He could do this. He smiled at her. Noticed how pretty she looked sitting there. "Just seemed like it might be nice to wind down."

"It would be," she admitted, that edge back in her voice.

"Talk to me," he said. "I used to be a good listener."

"Don't do that," she said.

"What?"

"Say 'used to be' like you're not a decent man," she said. "You lost the woman you loved and you are still recovering from that. In no way does that make you weak."

Her words cut to the core and he realized that he hadn't felt good in a long time. He knew that part of it was the resentment he'd felt toward Gill when she'd died. That sense of being abandoned. That sense of being left alone to raise Sofia. That sense that he wasn't sure how to live again.

***

Mads was back in her kitchen and Iona was determined this time he wouldn't leave her alone and wanting. Before, that had been acceptable. She was trying to understand how difficult it must be for him to move on with anyone. But after talking to her brother and her realization earlier tonight, she knew she wanted and needed more.

She wanted him.

"Thank you for that," he said.

"No problem. I've seen you with your daughter, with your brother, with the people who work for you. You're a good man, Mads. Don't forget it."

"That's the easy part. It's this that I keep screwing up at," he said, gesturing to the two of them and taking a long swallow of his drink.

"Why?" she asked. She had been careful, or as careful as she could be, not to push him towards anything …

"I want more from you," he said.

"Me too," she admitted.

"Well, that's a start," he said, putting down his glass as he came around the island.

"Is it?" she asked.

"It can be," he said, putting his hand on her waist and drawing her closer to him.

She closed her eyes, he smelled of Baileys and aftershave. Way better than she'd remembered.

He put his other hand on the back of her neck. It was big and warm, holding her gently. She felt the brush of his breath over her cheek and opened her eyes to see he was very close to her.

His blue-grey eyes weren't as icy as she always thought they were. There was a fire in them that called to her. Called to something deep inside of her that she'd been ignoring for a long time.

He didn't say anything, just looked down at her with that unfathomable look in his eyes as he rubbed his thumb over her lower lip. Tingles spread down her body, her breasts felt fuller and she stood up taller, leaning towards him for that kiss she wanted. But he took his time.

He reached up, tugging the elastic ponytail holder from her hair and she shook her head as he tossed it aside. He turned back to her, wrapping a strand of her hair around his hand.

"It almost looks like a flame," he said.

She reached up to touch his thick curls. He looked like a fallen angel. The kind that tempted humans into behaving in ways they shouldn't. But as he'd said, tonight it was just them. She turned off her brain. Stopped thinking about all the reasons why this might be a bad idea and just ran her hand down the strong column of his neck.

Just let her hands trace the edge of his sweater, where it met his skin, and then to dip below it.

He lifted her off her feet and put her on the counter top, pushing her legs apart so he could stand between them. She wrapped her arms around his shoulders and leaned down to kiss him. Their lips met and it was as if no time had passed since that kiss in the hallway. The passion he'd stirred in her then was reawakened and she plunged her tongue between his lips into his mouth.

He angled his head to allow her deeper access. She felt his hands on her back, sliding up under her pajama top. His hands were warm and smooth as he caressed her. She shifted against him, as he drew his nail down her spine.

She pulled her head from his and he looked up at her, she noticed his eyes were half-closed and she fought to keep her mind silent. To keep her fears locked away, but it was hard not to wonder if he knew he was kissing her or if he was remembering Gill.

She pushed him back and hopped off the counter. He pulled her off-balance back into his arms and he didn't say a word, but their eyes met and she knew he saw her. That she was the one he wanted tonight.

He lifted her off her feet again and carried her out of the kitchen, through the little hallway that led to her living room. He laid her down on the couch and then came down over her, his knee next to her hip, one arm under her shoulder blades, his mouth coming down hers and this time she didn't allow anything other than the weight of his body on top of hers to matter.

***

Mads wanted her. Wanted to lose himself in her magic tonight. She made a mockery of his self-control and shone a light on the lies he'd been telling himself. Her tongue tangled with his and driving ache for her took over him.

He tore his mouth from hers, felt the brush of her breath against his jaw and then her lips as she dragged them down his neck. He groaned as he hardened even more.

Her soft fingers ran down the side of his neck and she tapped her fingertip against the pulse that beat so strongly there. He wasn't fooling her. He was anything but cool tonight. He'd prided himself on being icy, on keeping his composure, but that wasn't something he could even pretend was happening anymore.

He shifted her in his arms, saw the outline of the swell of her cleavage in the opening of her top and leaned down, putting his head between her breasts and breathing in the warm scent of Iona. He felt her heart beating against her skin and knew she wanted him too.

Her back arched and the fabric cover over her breasts slipped until he saw the darkness of her nipple and leaned down to nuzzle it. He captured the tip between his lips and sucked it into his mouth.

Her hands plunged into his hair, holding him to her, her fingers rubbing against his scalp as she made little noises in the back of her throat.

"Mads ..." His name was a moan on her lips as her hands moved down to trace the shell of his ear and fondle the lobe before moving lower to his neck, tracing his Adam's apple with her nail.

Wedging her hand between their bodies, he felt her on his lower belly. Her cool fingers snaking between the fabric and popping one of his buttons until she pushed her fingers in there, rubbing them over his stomach.

His hips jerked forward at the first brush of her hand on his skin. He lifted his head from her breast and shifted back, his thighs resting on his heels. He caught the bottom hem of her shirt with two fingers and pulled it up over her head, tossing it aside.

Her skin was pale ivory with no freckles. Her waist was tiny and nipped in, her breasts beautiful and full and she just lay there and let him look at her.

Then she reached up and flicked open his other buttons on his shirt and he shrugged out of it. Before straddling her body and slowly lowering his chest until he could lightly rub it over hers.

She moaned again. Making that sound that he was fast becoming addicted to. A part of him wanted to pretend the attraction was just lust but there was no denying the magic that was Iona. She called to something in his soul that he could no longer deny.

He didn't have to pretend to want her. Every breath he took was filled with the cinnamon scent of her skin.

He put one hand in her hair, careful not to tug too hard on it, but he needed to hold onto her. He'd said it earlier, but her hair was like a flame … actually Iona was the flame and she was melting parts of him that he'd never realized he needed to thaw.

Tonight she was a fire that was burning him all the way to his core. Her head fell back, exposing her neck and he kissed it. Nibbled up and down the length until he turned his head and their lips met again.

She thrust her tongue deep into his mouth and he groaned in the back of his throat. She rocked up against him with the same rhythm as his tongue, as her thighs rubbed along the sides of his.

He was fascinated with each of her reactions and he could easily see himself becoming addicted to this … to her. More so than anything else he'd experienced for a very long time.

He shoved that thought aside. Right now he wanted her spread out under him. He needed her naked because he wanted all of her. Everything that Iona had to give him.

He just needed to be inside of her. To prove to himself that he wasn't as lost as he had been the last few years.

Damn.

He shut down his mind and just stared at her long slim legs and the feminine mysteries between them. She deserved better than him. He knew that but he knew he wasn't going to be able to make himself leave again.

"You take my breath away," he said. He couldn't give her words of love but he could tell her how much she meant to him.

He ran his fingers up her thighs, drifting higher until he reached the waistband of her pajama bottoms. He drew it slowly down, her body shifting back as he did so until she kicked them off and he tossed them aside. She wore a minute pair of bikini panties that were red.

"Wait, you'll love these," she said.

"I already do," he admitted, unable to tear his gaze from her body as she shifted around until her back was to him. She was on her knees, her red hair hung down her back and she looked over her shoulder at him.

His breath caught in his chest and he just stared at her. Until she shook her hips and he noticed that emblazoned across the back of her underwear was the word NAUGHTY.

He laughed and then reached for her, pulling her back into his arms. Her back to his chest and he rested his head on her shoulder as he skimmed his hands over the curve of her waist and then lower to the elastic of her naughty panties.

She put her hand over his and directed his hand inside of them, until he cupped her secrets. He gently caressed her. Her hips rotated against his erection, which strained against the front of his jeans. Using his free hand he undid the button and lowered his zipper, then adjusted his underwear until he was free of the cloth.

He touched her gently in a circular motion and she moaned. A sound of approval. He continued to move his fingers over her until she turned in his arms, her mouth finding his before she pulled back, shifting around until she got her panties off.

Her brown eyes were blazing with desire. There was a rosy pink flush to her skin and she breathed heavily, causing her breasts to rise and fall rapidly.

He stood up. He had a condom. Just the one. He'd tucked it into his pocket before grabbing the Baileys and coming down to her apartment.

He'd wanted her. No point in denying it.

She smiled when she saw it. He dropped down onto his knees, naked now, next to her. She reached for him and helped him put the condom on.

Sensation shivered down his back and he moved her hand off him. Before putting his hands on her thighs and pushing them apart. Her arms came around him and her thighs wrapped around his hips. He leaned down to catch her mouth with his, shifted his hips until he was poised to enter and then thrust into her.

He sucked her tongue deeper into his mouth. Letting her body adjust to his.

He held her hips as he drove himself into her, harder and harder, until she screamed his name.

He held her hips hard against his and thrust until an unstoppable orgasm raced through his body. He collapsed against her and felt her wrap her arms around his shoulders, he heard the beat of her heart and he pretended it was sweat from sex that caused his eyes to burn, but he realized he was crying. Just a few tears that he pretended he didn't feel.

Chapter 11

Iona held Mads in her arms and listened to the faint sound of music coming from the kitchen. Diana Krall singing *Have Yourself a Merry Little Christmas*. The jazzy sound of her voice gave the song a bluesy feel and suited the way she felt right now.

Sex had changed everything for her. Making her very aware that the relationships she'd had in the past had been almost superficial. There hadn't a man who'd made her feel what Mads had just now.

But Mads hadn't looked up at her since he'd come and she was holding on to him a little too tightly. She knew it so she forced herself to rub her hand up and down his back. He turned his head and she felt his lips lightly brush over the curve of her breast and then he shifted as he dropped kisses along her sternum. She felt a tiny tremor go through her at the feel of his lips on her skin and the abrasion of his beard stubble against her.

She kept running her hands up and down his back, letting her nails scrape against his skin gently. Finally, he shifted his arms under her and lifted himself up to look down at her. He seemed as if he wanted to say something but instead he just rested his forehead against hers, one of his arms going under her body, which forced her to arch her back, brushing the tips of her breasts against his chest. She realized, as physically satisfying sex with Mads had been, she still felt empty. Maybe because they hadn't really connected. She knew he was hiding something from her.

Complicated.

He was never going to be easy. He had more baggage than most men and she knew that before she'd invited him into her place tonight.

She wanted him again. Even now. As he was touching her and caressing her. It felt different this time.

He buried his hands in her hair as he looked into her eyes. He started to say something, but then stopped.

As he stared into her eyes she realized that she wished she could read his expression. Was it grief that had led him to hide what he felt? Or had he always been like that?

She didn't know. She doubted he was going to tell her and even if he did, she had no idea if it would be the truth or not. She shifted away from him.

Mads put his hand on the back of her neck, gently. Then she felt him lifting her up. He carried her down the hall, through her bedroom, and into the bathroom, where he set her on her feet. He turned his back to her and knelt next to the tub, adjusting the taps until the water was flowing out of them. She took off her top too. She walked over to the tub.

She reached over his shoulder for the bath salts and the foaming bath cube and dropped them into the tub. He didn't say a word, just held his hand out to her to help her into the water and then he climbed into the tub with her too.

She felt calmer than she had in a long time. She'd needed Mads more than she'd thought she would.

***

Mads guessed Iona knew that he'd thought of Gill at the end of making love to her and he hadn't meant to hurt her that way. As soon as he'd seen those tears in her eyes, everything else had dropped away. He might have been thinking about himself and his own grief, but in that moment he'd realized how much he truly was starting to care for Iona and he never wanted to see her in pain.

The bath was relaxing. The warm water was easing away some of the tension he'd been carrying around all week. He caught her foot and put it in the center of his chest and then took the loofah she had on the side of the tub and washed her leg. He was sitting up straight so that the spigot didn't dig into his back. But he wasn't uncomfortable at all.

"What do you have on next week?" he asked.

"Well the 'naughty and nice' truffle release. There's a sweet caramel truffle and a spicy Mexican hot chocolate-inspired one."

Mads shook his head ruefully. "She's earned the 'naughty' moniker now. But then so have you."

She gave him a half smile but he wanted to see that light back in her eyes. Wanted to see that magic he associated with her.

"I couldn't believe it when Hoop brought her into the apartment. I was freaking out but tried to stay calm. I knew if I freaked it would make her upset. And I could tell she was just about holding it together."

"You handled it great. Better than me," he said. "When you called I was about to go through the roof. I was only able to remain calm because of you. You're good for me."

"Am I?" she asked.

He put her leg back in the water and lifted her left one to wash it. "Yes."

"Where did you get this scar?"

He looked down at her toe, which she was rubbing over his pec. "Gill had an … outburst when she got the news she was terminal and started throwing stuff. I tried to get to her to comfort her and a glass shard cut me."

"Oh, Mads."

110

She pulled her foot back and scooted forward to straddle his lap, wrapping her arms around his shoulders. She hugged him close. He knew she meant for the embrace to be soothing and it was but she was naked and pressed to him like that he felt himself stir. This time not because he wanted to have sex so he could move forward but because of Iona. Because of how she always reached out to comfort him with no thought of her own emotional wellbeing.

He hugged her back.

"I'm sorry, I shouldn't be talking about another woman with you."

"Don't be silly." She put her hands on his face again and looked down into his eyes. "We can't hide from it."

"I know that," he admitted.

"Good."

He ran his hand down her back to distract him from her breasts, which were brushing against his chest. The tips of them were hard and rubbed against him when the water moved around them. He wanted this bath to be a peace offering but he wanted her again.

This time felt different.

She shifted a bit on his lap and took the loofah, rubbing it over his chest. "Want to stay with me?"

He did. More than anything. "I would like that a lot. But I am going to have to leave before morning."

"I know, you have to get home for Sofia."

"Yes, I do," he said. "Is that okay?"

"Of course, it is," she said. Then she stood up and water cascaded down her body. He tipped his head back to look at her. Her long slim legs, the nest of red hair at the top of her thighs, her nipped-in waist and her generous breasts and then higher to that sweet mouth, which smiled down at him. And he knew that he'd fixed his earlier mistake. And something shifted and settled deep inside of him. That thawing part of his emotional heart thawed a little bit more and though he knew that this wasn't the all-clear, he was closer to being able to start living again than he'd been in the last year.

He stood up next to her and they took turns drying each other off and then he lifted her in his arms again because he liked carrying her. She wrapped her arm around his shoulder as he carried her into the bedroom and placed her in the center of her bed.

***

Her hair had a slight curl to it when it was wet. It was spread out on the pillows, contrasting with the snowy white duvet on her bed. Her legs were slightly parted, her arms fell to her sides and he stood there staring down at her, knowing that this time he wanted to make it last. But having talked to her and knowing her so much better after the bath, self-control was further from him than it had ever been before.

He was hard, his erection stiff and desperate to be back inside the warmth of her body.

"Mads?"

He sat on the edge of the bed, facing her. He wanted to touch her, to know her body as well as he was coming to know her gentle soul, sweet heart, and feisty attitude. He wanted to take his time. But lately, when had he gotten what he wanted, he'd somehow lost control of everything that he'd once taken for granted.

He ran his finger over the breast closest to him. Lightly stroking the full globe and watching as her nipple tightened. He leaned down and licked it, gently. She made a little sound, more a catch in the back of her throat, and her hand fell to his head and then to his shoulder. He took the tip between his lips and sucked until he felt the bed move as her hips arched. He lifted his head and turned to kneel over her, using his thigh to push her legs further apart before settling between them. He was careful to keep his weight on his elbows as he brushed his chest over the hard tips of her breasts. She arched again, exposing her neck and he leaned down to lick and nibble at the length of her wet hair before tangling one of his hands in it as he bit lightly at the lobe of her ear. He shifted his hips until he felt his tip at the entrance of her body and this time he looked down into her eyes as he entered her as slowly as he could.

He pushed himself fully inside of her and stopped for a minute just to watch her adjust to him. She shifted under him, taking him deeper and her lips parted as she lifted her head up towards his. Their lips met and he started moving in her. She wrapped her arms around his shoulders and her legs around his hips as he thrust into her.

He put one arm under her hips, lifting her so he could go deeper and deeper. He drove them both hard towards their climax and he heard her gasp as she tore her mouth from his and called out his name once more.

Then he buried his face in the curve of her neck, driving harder, thrusting until he came. He emptied himself into her body and then rolled to his side, taking her with him. No guilt riding him this time. No regrets from wishing he could have been present for her. Just the feeling of having made love to a woman who was coming to matter more and more to him with each day.

He stroked his hand down her back as she curled on her side next to him and he held her to him. He realized he was holding himself a little tense, waiting for some emotional bomb from the past to spring on him but nothing happened. Just that feeling of contentment that came from making love to Iona.

He felt her drop a kiss on his chest and looked down at her. He didn't feel that wrenching guilt which had surprised him before.

He knew he'd been closed off for a long time and he wanted

to let her in … well, sort of, but he didn't know if he could.

It was funny for him to realize that this woman, who he'd only met at the beginning of December, was coming to mean so much to him. That she probably knew him better than anyone else did. He wasn't sure how he felt about that. He knew there were no guarantees for the future. Hell. He wasn't ready to think about that part of caring for a woman again. He might lose her like he lost Gill.

Damn.

Now that the thought had entered his head, he couldn't shake it.

"When do you have to leave?" she asked.

He sat up and looked at the clock on the nightstand. He should be home before five so he had time to shower before Sofia got up. "I can stay for a little while if you want me to."

"I'd like that," she said. "I would love to cuddle and just pretend that we are those two people with no past or future to worry about."

He propped the pillows behind his head and drew her into his arms. Then snagged the end of the duvet and pulled it over the both of them. He told himself that she was just doing what he'd suggested but he knew he wanted them to be Mads and Iona. Two people who might have a chance at something. Not two ships passing in the night, as he'd previously suggested.

But he didn't know how to tell her he wanted that without making it seem like he was ready for more than he knew he was.

Chapter 12

The High Line wasn't that busy early the next morning when she went to meet Cici and Hayley. They found a bench with a nice view of the city. Cici had brought along pain au chocolat from Sant Ambrose and mochas for all of them. The snow had let up and the three of them sat close together on the bench sipping their drinks.

"So …" Cici said, the steam from her mocha fogged up her glasses and her friend took them off to clear them.

"So?" Iona asked. She wasn't sure where to start when it came to Mads.

"Um … you showed up at the party alone last night, for starters," Hayley said. "Then a little girl arrives by herself and asks for you and then Hottie Mcbody shows up and you're not sure what we want to know about?"

She smiled at Hayley calling Mads Hottie Mcbody. "Okay. I know what you are curious about, but I'm not sure where to begin."

"Start with the hottie," Cici said. "He was very sweet on the couch with you and his daughter but when he looked at you, I could tell there was more going on there."

"Well, you know he's the CEO of Loughman Hotel Group.

We do need to finish that discussion and give him an answer, by the way."

"I'm leaning towards no," Hayley said. "I don't like the idea of training chefs to do what I do instinctively. I'm not saying I'm the only one who could do it but the three of us have a vision for the Candied Apple and it's not something I think other chocolatiers will automatically get."

"Fair enough," Cici said. "I have run some numbers that might change your mind, but let's discuss that back in the office. I want to hear about Mads and Iona."

Mads and Iona.

Her heart beat a little faster at the thought of them as a couple. They were sort of friends but still both were guarded.

"His wife — Sofia's mom — died last year on December 27. So, he's dealing with the first holiday without her. And Sofia doesn't believe in Santa but I think she wants to and it's just complicated."

"It makes sense if her mommy died at Christmas. She probably would have asked Santa to make her better," Hayley said. "I know I was sixteen when my mom got diagnosed and I prayed a lot and asked Santa to help her too."

Iona thought about all that the three of them had been through together. How she'd always known with them by her side she would survive anything. She wanted something more from Mads than just friendship. And she realized she'd been hedging her bets with him. Trying to protect herself from caring too much for him or even for Sofia.

She couldn't keep on doing that.

Hayley wrapped her arm around Iona's shoulders. "That sounds like a lot to take on."

"I know. I've tried to keep my distance but it's so hard not to fall for the two of them. Sofia is so precious and I think she really needs me. You've seen how she keeps coming around the shop."

"Yes," Cici said. "That's what I mean. Be careful about getting involved with her dad. If you sleep together and break it off … she might get hurt and she's already lost one mother."

Too late, she thought. "I would never cut her out of my life."

"He might be the one to do it," Hayley said.

"I know that too." Iona admitted that was one of her biggest fears.

Cici hugged her and then she felt Hayley's arm still around her. These women were more than friends to her. They were her sisters, in a way, and she was so grateful for them. "He was determined to make it a good evening for both of us, but in my mind, there is always Gill hanging around."

She hugged her friends and then got to her feet to go toss out her mocha, which was getting cold from the temperature. "Thanks, guys. I think I've been afraid to really let myself be involved."

"We know you have," Cici said. "You've driven us from the moment we had the idea to get the store open and running and then you spearheaded the marketing so we could be as successful as we are today. You put everything into the Candied Apple Café."

"I have," she admitted. "Theo thinks I'm trying to prove something to my father."

"I think so too," Hayley said. "You know how my dad is, so I get it. But you're much better now. I mean, you said we could all take Saturday off to go to the New York Ballet *Nutcracker* performance."

"Ha," Iona said, knowing Hayley was teasing her. "I didn't mean you could have the entire day off."

They laughed and joked before going their separate ways and Iona looked out at the City, remembering all the lessons her father had taught her. She knew how to run a campaign, how to lure investors and how to keep her company running a profit. But he'd never taught her how to balance both and until she'd met Mads and Sofia she hadn't considered that a liability.

Sofia had her headphones on when he got home from work that evening. Jessie had already given her dinner and then had plans with friends for the evening, so she'd waved goodbye as he'd walked in the door. He'd resisted the urge to text Iona. He'd gone to her last night and he didn't want to seem like he was coming on too strong.

It had been a long time since he'd dated or even thought about a woman the way he was thinking about Iona and he didn't want to come across as too needy.

Maybe getting involved with a woman at the first Christmas he'd been single wasn't the best idea.

He sat on the couch next to his daughter, reading work emails, but not really paying attention to them.

"Papa?"

He glanced over at Sofia, who had put her headphones on her lap and closed her tablet. "Yes."

"What are our holiday traditions?" she asked.

Where was this coming from, he wondered? They hadn't really had time to establish many traditions with Sofia before Gill had gotten sick. "Well … I don't think we have any, Sof. Do you want to start some?"

She crossed her arms over her chest and tipped her head to the side, considering things, he knew from past experience. "I think so. This is the first Christmas without Mommy and all."

"It is," he said, watching her carefully. Most of the time she seemed okay emotionally, but Mads felt like this was something new. He scooted closer to his daughter on the couch. "I'm afraid I don't know where to start with traditions. Uncle Piers and I used to make strings of popcorn for the tree with our mom when we were little. Do you want to do that?"

"We don't even have a tree," she pointed out.

"Want to get one?" he asked. In Christmases past, they'd spent most of their time at the hospital and had a tabletop ceramic tree that had painted-on ornaments and lights.

She nodded. "I think I would. Is that okay?"

He hugged her close and dropped a kiss on the top of her head. "Of course, it is. Let me Google where we can get a tree and we'll go get one."

"Tonight?"

"Why not? We don't have to be anywhere until tomorrow afternoon for the *Nutcracker*," he said.

"I can't wait for that. Jessie took me to get a new dress today."

"I know," he said. "Do you want to model it for me?"

"No, I'll wait until tomorrow," she said. "I want to get a tree."

He took out his phone and searched for a Christmas tree lot and found there was one not too far from their apartment building, but they were closed. "We will have to go in the morning. How about tonight we go and look at the shop windows on Fifth Avenue?"

"Can Iona go with us?"

"We can ask her. She might be busy," he said.

"She might not be," Sofia said. "I'll go and ask her."

"Get ready first so we go whatever she says."

"Yay!" Sofia said, skipping out of the room to her bedroom. She came back a few minutes later wearing her coat, stocking cap and holding her mittens.

"I'm ready."

"I can see that."

Mads put on his coat and then held the door open for his daughter. They walked slowly down the hall toward Iona's apartment, Sofia talking the entire time, telling him about the traditions of her classmates. Even Remy had traditions, Sofia informed him. Though given that he was so annoying they probably weren't good ones.

He stopped in front of Iona's door, looking at the cheerful wreath and remembering last night, when he'd stood in the same spot with a bottle of Baileys in one hand. Sofia knocked on the door before he could stop her.

He suddenly wished he'd said no when she'd suggested inviting Iona. But he knew that Sofia was trying to get through this first Christmas the same way he was. The one without Mommy. And if he had to see the woman who was making him feel all sort of emotions that he wished he could deny having, then he'd do it.

The door opened and Sofia waved at Iona.

"Hi! Papa and I are going to look at the Christmas windows, wanna come?" Sofia asked.

Iona stooped down to Sofia's level and gave his daughter a warm smile. "I'd love to. Let me grab my coat and purse and I'll be ready to go."

"Okay," Sofia said.

Iona left the door open as she stepped back inside and a few minutes later she was back wearing her Santa hat with the jingle bell on it, a red wool coat, and a pair of boots. She stepped out of her apartment, closing the door and checking that it was locked, and took Sofia's hand as they walked towards the elevators.

Mads followed after them, trying to tell himself that this was for Sofia so it didn't matter that Iona hadn't looked him in the eye. But he knew it did matter. Last night had changed something inside of him. And as much as he wanted to pretend that it had simply been another milestone that was helping to heal his grief from being alone, he knew that it was more.

That he wanted Iona's smiles to be directed at him as well as at Sofia. He didn't want her coming along to talk only to his daughter. And he knew that he could either just follow behind them, as she clearly intended for him to do, or he could remember the man he'd been before Gill had gotten sick.

When they all stepped out of the building, he took Iona's free hand in his and led the way toward Fifth Avenue.

"Do you mind walking?" he asked. "It's such a nice evening."

"Not at all," Iona said, looking pointedly at their joined hands and then back at him.

He just smiled at her. Let her guess at his intentions. He had no clue what was going on behind her pretty brown eyes.

Chapter 13

Snow covered the ground in Central Park as they walked through it to get to Fifth Avenue. It was pretty and cold but Iona concentrated on Sofia's talking instead of the fact that Mads was holding her hand like he wasn't going to let go. She had been unsure how to proceed. Had made up her mind to go all in with whatever was going on between the two of them. But thinking she'd do that and actually putting it into action were two very different things.

"Do you have any traditions, Iona?" Sofia asked. "Papa and I don't have very many."

Iona didn't find that hard to believe. "I do. One is going to the *Nutcracker* which we are all doing tomorrow."

Sofia smiled up at her. "That can be one for us too, Papa."

"Of course," Mads said. "What else do you do?"

"Well, I bake cookies and take them over to the E/C retirement home."

"What's the E/C?"

"Episcopalian and Catholic retirement home. They have an evening where they sing carols, so I usually put on my Santa hat, bring over cookies and join them."

"That sounds like fun," Sofia said.

Iona looked over at Mads. "It's always the Saturday before Christmas. This year that's the twenty-third. You're welcome to stop by," Iona said, although she didn't want to put any pressure on Mads to go.

"I think we'd like to go with you."

"That would be nice," Iona said.

They had gotten to the first holiday window on Fifth Avenue. Sofia made her way forward for a closer look, but Mads caught Iona's hand, holding her back.

"I have a Loughman Group holiday dinner next Thursday evening and um … most of the staff will be bringing a date, would you like to come with me?"

She looked at him in the sparkling glow of the Christmassy window and nodded. "I'd love to."

Sofia came back then and they took their time walking past the different windows, all with a holiday-themed vignette displayed in them. Sofia switched to walk between Iona and Mads, holding their hands. When they got to the Candied Apple, Iona noticed the shop was doing a fair amount of business for this time of night. And the hot chocolate they served was popular with the crowds of people who were out checking out the holiday windows and doing some last-minute shopping.

"Any one feel like some cocoa?"

"Me!" Sofia said, dropping Iona's hand and dashing into the shop. She followed behind her, aware that Mads' phone was ringing.

She glanced over at him.

"Go ahead and take that. I'll get our drinks and find us a table."

"Thanks," he said.

She went into the shop, very aware that she was hiding from him. She wondered if this was part of the problem she'd had with her past relationships. She did tend to keep a part of herself back. Maybe it was fear that she'd end up in a relationship like her parents, where they'd been strangers who shared a home and a bed. She'd always wanted more but had never really been able to figure out how to get it.

Sofia was looking at the different chocolates on display as Iona talked to Nick, who had proven himself in the shop and was one of their top salespeople for the holiday season. He had an easy smile for everyone and the customers really responded to him.

"Checking up on me, boss lady?"

"Not at all. Just enjoying this December night," she said. "I'll have three cocoas and are there any sugar cut-out cookies left?"

"I've got three Santa heads," he said.

"I'll take them. How's business?"

"Good. We are getting a mix of locals and tourists. Everyone is out tonight because of the snow earlier today. At night, it sparkles and makes everything seem more magical."

"It does, doesn't it?" she said.

"My favorite kind of night," he said.

Hers too, she realized. But she knew a big part of it was due to the company she was keeping. She took the tray with the cocoas and cookies on it to the table near the back that Sofia had put her hat and mittens on. But Iona couldn't find the little girl at first, but then noticed she was talking to a family with two boys a few tables away.

Iona put the tray on the table and turned to join Sofia when she saw the little girl was coming back to her.

"Who was that?"

"Remy and his brother," she said.

"The boy you had to give the apology chocolates to?"

"Yeah. His mom was really nice. She liked the candy so they came here tonight," Sofia said.

"Hayley does a really good job with the truffles," Iona said.

"I guess."

"What's the matter?" Iona asked, helping Sofia take off her coat and getting her settled in her chair.

"Nothing."

Iona took off her own coat and sat down next to Sofia. "Did he say something mean to you?"

"No."

Iona got the hint and stopped asking questions, talking instead about cookies. "I have always loved sugar cookies like this with frosting on them."

"They're okay. Mommy couldn't have any kind of colored frosting," Sofia said.

"Do you want something else?" Iona asked.

"I think I want to go home."

"Okay. Let's get your coat on and find your dad."

Sofia stood up, bumping the table as she did so. The cocoa was jostled and spilled on the table and then Sofia looked at it and burst into tears. Iona knelt in front of the little girl and she just looked at her with her brown eyes full of tears and Iona had no idea what was really bothering her but just pulled her into her arms, hugging her close.

"I miss my mommy," Sofia said.

"I know, sweetie."

Sofia stood stiffly for a second and then hugged Iona back and soon she stopped crying. Iona got a napkin and handed it to Sofia to dry her tears. Nick came over and cleaned the table quickly, but as she stood up Iona noticed Remy watching Sofia and beyond him she saw Mads in the doorway looking unsure and upset.

Of course, he was. His daughter was crying in the middle of a candy store. Iona looked down at Sofia, who just took her hand and Iona led her over to her father. She didn't say anything to Mads as they left the Candied Apple Café.

***

Mads tucked Sofia in after reading her favorite story, the book

125

that she and Gill had made their own, and then came back into his living room, where Iona was waiting.

"What happened at the Candied Apple Café?"

"I'm not really sure. We were fine and then she saw the boy from school and something changed. She said he wasn't mean to her. But she didn't want to stay any longer," Iona said. "She started crying when she bumped the table, but I don't think it was the spilled drinks that had upset her."

Mads nodded. Of course, it wasn't. They'd never done anything like they had this evening with Gill. She'd always been too frail to be outside during the winter weather. "Are you sure the boy didn't upset her?"

Iona shook her head. "I really don't know. I was ordering our drinks and didn't get to go over to him or his parents."

This was what came of trying to do something different. Rationally, he knew that it wasn't the fact that they had been doing something Christmassy, but in his gut he felt like it was. Every time he tried to make it picture-perfect, something like this happened. "I'll ask the principal to set up a meeting for me with his parents. I'll see if I can get to the bottom of it."

He rubbed the back of his neck. He had been thinking when he'd been outside of the Candied Apple that maybe he and Sofia were both ready for someone new in their lives, but he wasn't sure now. His daughter usually seemed so even-tempered but lately something was going on with her, something he wasn't able to put his finger on or fully understand.

"She did say she misses her mommy," Iona said. "I mean, you probably already know that but I think there was something about seeing Remy and his family that made her think about her mom."

Of course she would. "Damn. I just don't know what to do about that. I talk to her and I'm here for her but I can't make a mom appear."

"No, you can't. I guess just keep doing what you're doing. Do you think my presence tonight is upsetting her?"

126

"I don't think so. She adores you. It was her idea to invite you to come along."

"Oh. So, you didn't want to see me?" she teased.

"Of course I did. I was giving you space," he said, admitting out loud what he'd been thinking.

"I don't need any space," she admitted.

"You make me feel alive again and that's not very comfortable. I thought I was in this safe cocoon where I would spend the rest of my life alone, but then you ran into me with your jingle-bell Santa hat and infectious smile and made me realize that I'm not."

Mads felt exposed and raw. He shouldn't have said as much as he had to her but with her things were different and all the charm he'd once thought he had was long gone. Watching the woman he loved die had burned all of that out of him. And he'd never thought he'd meet another woman he could feel anything for. And he wasn't saying this was love … he wasn't ready for that and he was pretty damned sure that Iona wasn't, but there was something between them.

"I know. I just want to make this easier for you both. And if I'm being honest, I really don't want to get hurt either."

"I don't want to hurt you," he admitted.

"Fair enough," she said. "Maybe we should take a breather. No more kissing or sleeping together, okay?"

Mads didn't think that was a good idea. But he wasn't about to say no to her. He liked Iona and the thought of doing anything to further hurt her wasn't something that he was willing to do.

"If that's what you want to do, then I'm in."

"I do," she said. "I think I'll go home now. I'll meet you both at Lincoln Center tomorrow afternoon."

"I don't mind if you ride with us," he said.

"Thanks. But I have to go by the Candied Apple in the morning and it will be easier to meet there."

"Okay. I'm taking Sofia to buy a tree tomorrow morning. Maybe you can help us decorate it?"

"If she wants me too," Iona said.

"What about what we want?"

She bit her lower lip. "I'm not sure what you mean?"

He wasn't about to lay himself bare for her. Not about to say that he wanted her with him because she made it easier to cope with this Christmas. She made his apartment feel less empty, made him forget that Gill wasn't here and if he was honest, that she never had been here. He hadn't realized until now that Gill's illness hadn't just taken away Sofia's belief in the magic of Christmas, but it had also seeped into their holiday celebrations until they'd had nothing to be joyful about at this time of year. And he wanted to find a way to give that back to his daughter and maybe find it for himself.

But those words weren't coming easily to him so he just shrugged and said goodnight to Iona, watching her as she left his apartment.

***

Getting the tree was easy enough, but once they got back he realized they didn't have any ornaments or lights.

"I'll go and get some of the basics while you two are at the ballet," Jessie said. "Do you want multi-colored lights or white?"

Mads wasn't sure. "Sof?"

"I think white, Papa. Will it look like snow?"

"I don't think so, squirt," Jessie said. "But it will be pretty and sparkly."

"Papa?"

"Jessie's right. I'm sure that the white lights will be nice," he said. "Do you want to go and look at some other trees before you decide?"

"I think so," Sofia said. "The tree lighting we went to was all colors."

"Yes, it was. But we have some trees at the Common that are

128

all white lights. It's really pretty. Why don't we plan to stop by after the ballet?"

"Okay," Sofia said.

"I'll hold off on buying anything," Jessie said as Sofia left the living room. "I know it's not my night off, but are you two going to be gone all evening?"

Mads nodded. "Yes. Do you want the night off?"

"If you don't mind. My boyfriend invited me to join him at a Christmas party. I was going to see if Sofia wanted to go, but it seems like you two will be busy."

"Thanks. Jessie, has she said anything to you about Gill?" Mads asked.

"No. Why?"

"She started crying last night while we were out looking at the Christmas windows on Fifth Avenue and said something to Iona."

"I'm sorry, Mads. She hasn't said anything to me. She's been off on the walks home from school lately. More quiet than usual and when she does ask questions they are about traditions and family. I didn't really think much of it. First grade is different than kindergarten was and she has been doing a lot of projects around the holidays."

Mads wondered if he needed to go talk to the principal. He'd already called her to discuss Remy and his family. But this might be something else. "Yes, they are. I guess all we can do for now is keep our eye on her."

"I will. You know I can cancel tonight," Jessie said.

"No, you can't. You haven't done anything for the holidays in six years. I think it's okay if you go to a party with your boyfriend," Mads said. All of them had been focused on making the most of the holidays with Gill while she had still been with them. Even Jessie. And the nanny deserved to enjoy this holiday.

"Are you sure?"

"Yes. And I'm the boss, so no arguing."

She stuck her tongue out at him but then came over and gave

him a hug. "Thanks."

"You're welcome. Enjoy your evening."

Jessie left the living room and Mads stared at the tree that Sofia had selected, which was large and full. It touched the ceiling and filled the window that overlooked Central Park. He'd paid extra for this apartment and the view.

Sofia needed family this year. She was searching for something and he hadn't yet figured out what it was, but he suspected she needed more than just the two of them.

He texted his brother but Piers didn't answer. His parents were both gone and it had been just him and Piers for the last ten years. He hadn't talked to Gill's parents since school had started. They lived in Northern California. He didn't like talking to them because they had had a difficult time dealing with Gill's illness and had checked out of their lives long before Gill had died. But maybe they would be there for Sofia.

He sent them an email asking them to come for Christmas. Now he just had to wait.

He went into Sofia's room after he got dressed in a suit and tie for the ballet and found his daughter at her desk, writing on a piece of paper with a large red marker.

"What are you working on?"

She covered the paper with her chubby little hands. "Nothing, Papa."

He held his hands up. She sometimes made him drawings for his office and never wanted him to see them until she was ready. "I won't peek. Are you ready for the ballet?"

"I think so. Would you be able to do a bun on the top of my head?" she asked. "Like a ballerina?"

"I don't know," he said. "Grab your tablet and come over here. We can Google it and I'll give it a try."

"Thanks, Papa."

"Why didn't you ask Jessie to do this before she left?" he asked her as she sat at the stool in front of her vanity. Their eyes met in the mirror.

"You said you liked learning new things," she reminded him.

"When did I say that?" he asked her.

"On the first day of school when I wanted to stay home."

He had said that to her. She had been afraid to leave him and go to school and he had wanted to hold onto her as well; keep her in his presence always so he knew she was safe. But he knew that wasn't healthy for either of them and he had done his best to encourage her to go to school.

"You're right, I did say that. But I was thinking of things like reading and math, not putting your hair in a ballerina bun."

"But this is more fun than math," she said with a smile and then started giggling. "I bet Uncle Piers doesn't know how to do this."

"Just one more thing I'm better at than him," he said with a smile.

"I wish I had a brother to be better than," Sofia said.

"Sof, do you really?" he asked.

"I know I can't because of Mommy."

She put on the video on YouTube that demonstrated how to make the bun but he couldn't stop thinking about what she said. He hadn't thought of their family beyond the two of them. Sure, he liked Iona and wanted to see her again but another child … another wife? He wasn't sure he'd ever have the courage to let anyone else into his heart again.

Chapter 14

Iona was running late. She wasn't sure what it was about December but she couldn't seem to get out anywhere on time this month. It was easy to blame the crowded city sidewalks with gawkers stopping to stare at the decorated Christmas windows of shops along Fifth Avenue, but she knew part of it was her.

She was moving slower. Not for any good reason other than she didn't want to be at the *Nutcracker* for the matinee family benefit this afternoon, though the ballet was one of her favorites.

She rounded the corner to the David Koch Center at Lincoln Center and realized all the hurrying in the world wasn't going to make her on time. There was a crowd of people waiting to get inside the venue. She glanced up at the sky. It was clear and very cold this afternoon. Not a single cloud in the sky to bring on some snow.

As a girl, before she got too tall and developed curvy hips, she'd dreamed of being a ballerina. Truth was, she'd never really had the dedication that was needed as well as her genes not giving her the slim, svelte frame required. She'd liked the costumes and wearing her hair up in a tight bun. In fact, she'd dressed with that in mind this afternoon. Her hair up in a ballerina bun, her dress a fitted red velvet top with a cream satin underskirt and a layer of tulle over it.

She wore her black wool opera cape and as she edged closer to the doors she fumbled in her bag for her ticket.

"Iona?"

She glanced over her shoulder and saw Sofia and her father standing a few feet away. Sofia also had her hair up in a bun and she smiled and waved at Iona. Mads was on his phone, furiously tapping the screen. Probably giving some hapless employee a dressing down about not following his explicit instructions.

"Hello little one. Are you excited for the ballet?" Iona asked.

"Yes. I've never been before."

She edged away from her father and Mads stopped tapping his smart phone screen. "Sof."

"It's okay. I'll watch her while you finish up what you're doing."

Their eyes met and all she could think of was that moment when their lips had brushed each other, how he'd held her while she'd fallen asleep and then hadn't called her for two days. He reached into his pocket and pulled out two tickets. He handed one to Iona. "If you ladies want to wait inside, I'll catch up."

She glanced down at Sofia and saw the disappoint dash quickly across her face before she slipped her small hand into Iona's. "Okay, Papa."

She took Sofia's ticket and held it with her own as she rejoined the line to go into the David Koch Center. "What have you been up to since I saw you?"

"Not too much. At school, we learned about more Christmas traditions. Some of them are funny. In Italy, a witch delivers presents to children, not Santa, well, I guess probably Santa does it now."

"I think he does. I know the witch, though. Befana, right?" Iona asked. She'd dated an Italian once and his mother had one of those Befana dolls by the entrance of her home. "I think she keeps the evil spirits away."

Sofia giggled. "She does. Papa said his bad attitude did that for us."

Iona had to chuckle. "I totally agree with that."

They handed their tickets to the attendant and stepped inside the warmth of the lobby. "That's better. It was very cold outside. Let's get rid of our coats and then get something to drink."

Sofia kept her hand neatly tucked into Iona's as they got in line for the coat check and then made their way to the bar. "What would you like to drink? Peppermint hot chocolate or a jingle bell mocktail."

"What's a jingle bell mocktail?" Sofia asked.

Sparkling soda, grenadine, and frozen limeade mixed together and topped with a cherry. "Tastes like a cherry and lime soda."

"Peppermint hot chocolate," she said.

Iona ordered two of them.

"Make that three," Mads said, joining them. He reached around Iona to pay.

"Thanks for watching Sof for me," he said.

"No problem. We were talking about Christmas traditions," she said. "This is actually one of my family's."

"It is?" Sofia asked. "Are they here? Is your mom here? She was nice when I met her."

Iona smiled. Her mom had that effect on people. Her parents had been such an odd couple, she thought. Her mom gregarious and the life of the party; her father always in his study or at work. "She's looking forward to seeing you as well. She's somewhere in this crowd. We always come to this event since it benefits the New York City Ballet."

"Why?" Sofia asked.

Mads watched both of them and Iona realized she didn't mind sharing secrets with Sofia, but Mads made her want to keep her guard up. "I used to want to be a ballerina and Mom talked my father into making a donation and bringing us here every year."

"Sofia wants to be one too," Mads said.

The little girl smiled up at her. "That's why we both have ballerina buns. Where are we sitting?"

"Orchestra. My mom and brother and I usually meet over near the bar and have a toast first. This is my family's official 'it's Christmas' kick off," she said.

She felt a tiny hand slip into hers and looked down at Sofia, who had taken her hand gently.

"Is your brother nice?"

"Yes, he is. Why do you ask?"

"Papa doesn't always get along with Uncle Piers," Sofia said.

She glanced at Mads and saw him give his daughter a wry look. "There are no secrets with this one. My brother and I have always disagreed on how to run the hotel, so it makes any family get-togethers awkward."

"I could never work with Nico. He's great, but he has a completely lax work ethic."

"You must be talking about me," her brother said from behind her.

Mads put his hand on the small of her back as she turned to face her brother and his new fiancé.

***

There were many situations that Mads had faced in his time at the head of the Loughman Group. Iona smiled and gave her brother an air kiss on both cheeks and then did the same for the man standing next to him.

He knew that Iona had once fancied herself in love with Nico, so he was trying to see what she might have seen in him. Even being objective he could see that the other man had classic good looks. Dark hair, strong jaw line, but Mads noticed that his hairline was receding slightly and that his grin was too big and his teeth too perfect.

"These are my friends Mads and Sofia," Iona said. "This is

my brother Theo and his fiancé Nico."

Mads reached around her to shake both men's hands and Sofia just waved hi to them, moving to stand between him and Iona. She was okay with meeting new people most of the time. But he knew she felt protective of Iona and wasn't going to be overly friendly to her brother.

"Mom sent me to try to find you," Theo said.

"The line to get in was crazy."

"It was. We got here early so that I could show Nico all the places where we used to take photos with Dad," Theo said.

"We were just on our way," Mads said. "I had to finish up a business call and then we were going to try to get a photo in front of the Christmas tree in the lobby."

"I'll take it for you," Nico said.

Mads hadn't really planned on taking a picture, it had just slipped out. He didn't have any photos with himself and Sofia with anyone other than his wife. But he wanted to remember this afternoon with Sofia and Iona.

"Will you take it with my phone?" Iona asked, opening her clutch and pulling it out. "I'll send it to Mads later."

Nico took the phone from Iona and Mads felt a little bit queasy. This was it. Another first. One of the things he'd been dreading. It wasn't like Gill was going to be upset that he was in a picture with Iona and Sofia. She was done being upset about anything. She was in another place and she had said they should move on.

But he wasn't ready. Not really. Not prepared for any of this. Everyone on the board had thought he was so strong when he'd come right back to work after the funeral. He'd been complimented about how well he'd adjusted, but in his heart, he knew he hadn't adjusted at all.

Sofia didn't seem to notice anything, skipping ahead of him and Iona toward the big Christmas tree in the center of the lobby. And when they got closer Iona took his arm at the elbow and drew him to a stop. She reached up as if she were adjusting his tie and leaned in close to him. She smelled of peppermint and chocolate.

"You don't have to do this," she said. "I can take one with Sofia."

He touched the side of her face. Wondered when it had happened that she'd gone from the lady down the hall to Iona, his friend. And they were friends now, but — and maybe this was what bothered him so much about the photo — he knew he wanted more. He knew that if she indicated in any way that she was open to more than friendship; he'd jump at it.

"I have to," he said. "It's going to happen sooner or later and I'd rather it be with you."

Some emotions danced across her features, tightening them for a second, but then she smiled. "I'm glad. I want to remember this night and the magic that is Christmas."

"Christmas is magic," he said.

Even though he didn't believe it. Hadn't seen any miracles when he'd needed them. But he saw it on Sofia's face as she stared up at the tree decked in twinkling lights and *Nutcracker*-themed ornaments. He saw in Iona's smile, which wasn't forced now but natural. And he wanted to let her into his heart, but he couldn't. Not yet. But for the first time since Gill died he knew there was a chance that he could start to feel something again other than love for his daughter and pain and anger at the world.

And if that wasn't Christmas magic he didn't know what was.

"How should we do this?" Mads asked. There were families and couples all trying to get a photo by the Christmas tree.

"Like this," Theo said, coming over and positioning them. He put Mads in the back with Iona and Sofia in front of them. "Put your arm around Iona."

Mads did so and she shifted to lean into the curve of his body as Sofia leaned back against his legs. Iona tipped her head to the side as she started to smile, and he knew he was looking at her and not Nico when he took the first picture. But he couldn't help himself. There was a thought running through his head that Iona was the magic and not Christmas.

***

After the matinee performance of the *Nutcracker* everyone made their way down a hallway, where there was a meet-and- greet with the principals from the ballet and the adorable kiddos from the New York Ballet's charity event. Iona tried to keep her concentration on that instead of on Mads. He'd taken a photo with her and Sofia. She knew she shouldn't let it mean too much. He had said it was the first and there would be others. Probably he'd meant other women, but a part of her hoped that maybe for once her luck with men was changing. Maybe this time she wouldn't just fix the guy so he could find love but she'd fix him so he'd find love with her.

But that wasn't why she was with Mads. They were just two lonely souls who needed a friend. But the other night had changed things. They were lovers now. She'd been desperate not to be the only one of her friends alone when she'd agreed to the match-making thing … and look how that had turned out.

"Iona, take my picture with Sugarplum Fairy," Sofia said. The fairy went up on pointe as she put her arm lightly around Sofia's shoulder and the little girl beamed as Iona took the photo. The joy on Sofia's face reminded Iona that she'd lost that in the last few years. It was easy to say it was because her schedule was so busy or that she was just getting older, but another part of her knew it was because after her dad died she hadn't been able to properly let him go. To properly forgive him for all of the angst he'd caused her for so many years. Always being a little too judgmental with his praise and making her feel like she wasn't good enough.

"Do you want a photo with your daughter?" the man behind

138

her asked.

"She's not … yes, I'd like that," Iona said.

She posed with the ballerina and Sofia and then took her phone back from the man and they continued walking along toward the banquet room, where they'd have a meal. She didn't see Mads but then he'd said that there was a problem at work and he needed to deal with it. So, she expected he'd show up when he could. She wasn't as anxious about seeing Theo and Nico again. Mads had somehow, with his sweet gesture, made it possible for her to really start moving on.

She saw Hayley and Cici up ahead waving at her and Sofia waved back at them. "I can't wait to see baby Holly again. She's so cute."

"She is adorable. But so are you," Iona said, wondering if the little girl was jealous of sharing attention with the newborn.

"I know," Sofia said, letting go of her hand and skipping over to Hayley and Cici.

The last few months since everything had happened with Theo they'd started trying to cheer up, fearing she was working longer hours because of a broken heart. Which had been very sweet of them.

"Sorry about that," Mads said from behind her.

"It's okay. We've had a few photos … I'll text them to you and now Sofia is hoping to hold the baby."

"She told me last night when I tucked her in that she wants a brother or sister."

Iona heard the anguish in Mads' voice and she squeezed his hand. "Give it time. Right now, she can play with Cici's baby and maybe that will help."

"I hope so."

Sofia noticed Mads was back and even the thrill of maybe getting to hold the baby wasn't enough to keep her from running back to her father.

"Papa."

Iona noticed that she always ran to him when she saw him after he'd been gone. A part of her was always envious of how Mads would stop what he was doing and bend down to scoop up his daughter. He was the kind of father she'd longed for. And Iona was very happy that he was Sofia's daddy because he was perfect for the little girl.

"Sof. I heard you met everyone from the cast."

"I did. I even used my pretend sword to battle the Rat King."

"Did you win?"

"Of course, Papa. That's a silly question," Sofia said with a giggle. "I'm glad we are sitting at the table with baby Holly. Cici said she might let me hold her, if it's okay with you."

"If you promise to be very careful I think we could manage that."

"Yes. Let me go and tell her," Sofia said, squirming for Mads to put her down, which he did.

She ran back to Cici and Iona noticed her friend stooped down to be on eye level with Sofia, carefully holding the baby in her arms.

"I like your friends," Mads said.

"They are the best. Luckiest day of my life when I met them," she said.

"You'll have to tell me about it sometime. I'm jealous of how you can work together and maintain that friendship."

Iona knew he reported to the board, which was made up of many of his family members and his brother was the CFO, which meant they probably butted heads at times.

"The key is to let go of the small stuff."

"I'll try to remember that."

Chapter 15

The ballet had been on December 9th and since then Iona had been careful to keep her distance from Sofia and Mads. But neither of the Erikssons would let her. Sofia stopped by the Candied Apple Café after school with her nanny and talked to Nick the Wednesday after the ballet and apologized for spilling her cocoa. And then she played with Lucy, Hayley's rescue miniature dachshund in Iona's office while Jessie went to buy presents for Mads and Sofia.

"I told Papa we should get a dog, but he said that I needed to prove I could listen before we could get one," Sofia said.

She was sitting on the floor holding the miniature dachshund on her lap. The little dog was very patient with Sofia and had allowed her to tie a bow around her neck and had posed for several selfies with the little girl. Iona snapped a photo of her with Lucy and texted it to Mads, even though she was trying to keep her distance from him. But she knew he'd love to see his daughter smiling so broadly.

"That's a good idea. Dogs take a lot of work," Iona said. "She belongs to Hayley but Cici and I help watch her all the time. You can't just leave her alone for a long time."

"I know that. Miss Pembroke told us all about it. And that

141

sometimes Santa wouldn't bring you things you asked for if he didn't think you could handle it," Sofia said.

Iona smiled to herself. "What did she say after that?"

"Just that parents should be the ones buying a dog. You can't ask Santa for just anything."

Iona saved the document she'd been trying to work on and leaned forward. "Like what?"

"Anything your Papa can't get for you," she said. "He can't make sick people well. Papa said sometimes people want something so badly they de-something themselves."

"De-something?"

"I can't remember the word but it's like fool themselves," she said.

"Deceive?"

"Yeah, like that," she said.

"What's on your Christmas list?" Iona asked her, to change the subject. She hadn't taken the time to think about the reasons why Mads might have had to tell his daughter that Santa didn't exist. But hearing Sofia made her a little sad for both Sofia and Mads. She couldn't imagine what it would be like to disappoint this little girl. To not be able to tell her that everything was going to be okay. But being Sofia, she wouldn't expect that.

"I was going to ask for a dog, but now I think I'm going to ask for ballet lessons," she said.

"That's a good thing. What else?"

"Jessie said I can't ask for family members."

"What? What kind of family members do you want? You have your uncle and your grandparents, right?"

"Yeah, but I wanted a brother. Papa is so lucky to have Uncle Piers."

"He is lucky, but I don't know if your Papa is ready for another kiddo right now," Iona said gently.

"Do you think so?" Sofia asked.

"Yes. Plus, it sounds like fun having a brother but that means

142

that you have to share everything," Iona said.

"You like your brother, is that because you never had to share with him?" Sofia asked.

Iona realized she'd opened a can of worms. Why couldn't Sofia have just wanted a new doll or a bike? Iona was the first to admit she really wasn't too sure she understood what kids wanted and Sofia was teaching her a lot.

"Theo and I don't mind sharing, plus we like different things," Iona said. They had always been close. She was forced to admit that she missed talking to her brother since she'd been so busy at the Candied Apple Café. He'd been a part of her circle of friends not because of proximity but because he was more than just a relative. "I got my feelings hurt by something and have felt weird talking to him ever since."

Lucy jumped down from Sofia's lap and trotted towards the door. Sofia looked over at Iona.

"She might need to go outside. Want to come with me to take her?"

"Yes," Sofia said. "I feel that way about Remy. He's been pretty nice to me since I apologized."

Iona bent to put Lucy's leash on before opening the back door that led to the alley behind the Candied Apple. "His family seemed friendly."

Sofia shrugged. Iona wondered if she'd finally indicate what had upset her that night they'd run into them. But the little girl just stood in the doorway staring at the dog, which sniffed around to find the right place to do her business.

"He has a brother and a mommy," Sofia said softly.

Iona looked away from Lucy and back at Sofia. "Not every family has a mommy and daddy and brother or sister."

"I know that," Sofia said. "I know that my mommy is gone so that's why I didn't think about asking Papa for one."

"My friend Hayley doesn't have any siblings. It's just her and her dad."

"Really?"

"Yes. And then Cici has two half-brothers," Iona said. "There's not just one way a family can be. And sometimes your family can be people who aren't even related to you."

"Really?" Sofia asked. "Like who?"

"Cici and Hayley are like my sisters. We started out as friends and became much more."

"I don't have any friends like that," Sofia said.

"You have Jessie," Iona pointed out.

She nodded and then Lucy ran back to them and they took the dog back inside. Hayley offered to show Sofia how to use the chocolate mold to make candies and she went off to learn. Iona went back into the office, thinking more about her brother than she had allowed herself. She decided she'd take the evening off and then she texted Theo before she could change her mind and invited him to come over for dinner.

***

Mads saw the text from Iona when he was in the middle of a meeting and forced himself to ignore it until it was over. He had to smile when he saw his daughter holding Hayley's dog. Though Iona had been insistent that they should give each other some space, since the ballet they'd still been seeing each other a lot. And Sofia wasn't about to lose her new friend. She'd told him this morning that she wanted to be more like Iona.

He wasn't entirely sure what it was that she wanted to emulate but she had been smiling more often and he noticed that she seemed to be trying a lot of different holiday things. So far, they had established one new tradition. They read a different holiday book each night before Sofia went to bed. Some of them were religious-based, others were books about puppies or elves. And Sofia had enjoyed them all. He had ordered a few new ones that Amazon had delivered to his apartment that afternoon, so tonight they'd have some more to choose from.

His brother was flying in this weekend and they were going to take Sofia to see the Rockettes. One of the women that Piers used to date a few years ago had a friend who was in the show and had offered them tickets. So, they were going. Sofia hadn't cried again since the night they'd been out with Iona at the Candied Apple. But she had been dropping hints that she thought their family was too small.

He worried she might think that something would happen to him and she'd be all alone. So, he'd been on at Piers to come and visit more frequently. Which wasn't easy given he ran a hotel on the West Coast.

Lexi knocked on his door and then leaned in, "Call on line one. It's Sofia's school."

"Thank you. I'm sending a photo to the printer. Would you make sure there is printer paper in it?"

"Certainly."

She closed the door behind her and he picked up the call. "Mads Eriksson."

"Mr. Eriksson, this is Miss Pembroke, Sofia's teacher. I'm returning your call."

"Thank you," he said. "I just wanted to check in and see if Sofia was doing better in class after the incident with Remy."

He heard the shuffling of papers on the other end and used his thumb to flip through the saved pictures on his phone. He had two photos from Iona. One was of the three of them at the *Nutcracker*. He hesitated with his thumb over the delete button but he knew he couldn't get rid of it. That picture was … well, he wasn't deleting it. He pushed it aside and pulled up the photo of Sofia with the puppy and hit print.

"She hasn't gotten into any more arguments with anyone. She does seem a little lost when we get into the Christmas stuff. I've been helping to steer her towards finding the things that will work for her."

"What can I do?" Mads asked.

"She mentioned you were starting some traditions and I think that's a good place to start. Honestly, each child is different and most days Sofia seems pretty easy going and happy. Occasionally something will throw her off but I think you're doing everything you can for now," Miss Pembroke said.

That wasn't what he wanted to hear. He wished the teacher would give him a list of thing she could check off that would guarantee that Sofia would be able to get through Christmas and adjust to it. "Should I take her out of school and go on a vacation for the holidays?"

She sighed. "I really don't think that would help. She is already contemplating what's unique about Christmas. I think staying here will be better for her in the long run."

Mads couldn't really just leave the Common or New York City for a few weeks and he knew that. But for Sofia he would do what was needed. "Thank you for your time, Miss Pembroke. If anything changes, please call me."

"I will," she said.

She hung up the phone and Mads sat back in his chair, knowing there were no easy answers to parenting. It had been this way since Sofia had turned two and Gill had received her diagnosis. He'd been on his own dealing with every decision for their daughter and he had big shoulders, he could handle the weight of those decisions, but there were times when he just was so unsure of what to do with his daughter. He just wanted someone to talk to. Someone who wasn't Piers, who had even less of a clue about little girls than Mads did.

Iona might be able to help. Sofia spent a lot of time with her. Jessie was happy to give Mads her opinions but she was an employee, which she always pointed out. He opened the text conversation where Iona had sent him the photo of his daughter.

He started to type in there, asking her if she was free that evening, but in the end he just deleted the message. She'd asked him to give her space and he needed to respect that.

It didn't matter that he dreamt of her in the middle of the night when he couldn't control his thoughts. It didn't matter that sometimes he picked up his scarf and caught a whiff of her perfume on it. Or that he still remembered how her lips felt under his. He wasn't ready to commit to her, not like she needed him to.

And every time he thought of just reaching out he remembered the look on her face when she said she didn't want to be hurt again. And he knew that even though he'd been thinking that he wasn't stuck in stasis any longer, he was a long way from being able to care for Iona the way he knew she deserved to be cared for.

***

Iona checked her appearance in the mirror for the fifth time as she waited for Nico and Theo to show up. She was excited to see her family and realized she wanted Mads and Sofia to join them. But she didn't want it to be awkward, so she waited until the last minute to dash out of her apartment and down the hall to them.

There was a battery-operated light-up penguin with a Santa hat on their front door. She smiled as she noticed it. Slowly Sofia and Mads were figuring out what they liked and didn't like for Christmas and that made her feel good. She knocked on the door.

She waited a few minutes, during which she debated just going back to her place and waiting for her brother.

But then the door opened and it was Mads wearing an apron that read TRUST ME I'M THE COOK. He had a bit of flour on his chin and he was wiping his hands on a towel.

"Iona. We weren't expecting you tonight," he said. "You look very nice."

She smoothed her hands down the side of her sleeveless Ralph Lauren fit and flare dress. It was in a festive gold fabric and she'd pulled her hair up and taken her time with her make-up to ensure she looked her best.

"Thank you. I'm sorry I bothered you. I can see you're busy."

"It's okay," he said. "We aren't that busy. Won't you come in?"

"I can't. I am expecting Nico and Theo at any moment. I invited them over for dinner. And I thought it would be nice to have you two join us," she said. The words came out in a rush.

"Papa? Are you coming back?" Sofia called from the kitchen.

"In a minute, Sof. Jessie's in charge until I'm back," Mads said, beckoning Iona into the apartment. "Why are you coming to invite us just now?"

"I didn't want it to be awkward, like I'm introducing you to my family, but Sofia is the one who made me realize how lucky I am to have my brother, and instead of working every night I wanted to have a family dinner," she said.

"We already ate and are baking cookies, but we can come down once they are done," he said.

That sounded perfect to her. "That sounds good to me."

"Sofia was planning to bring you some anyway," he said.

"Okay. Sorry for the last-minute invite. This is so silly."

Mads shook his head. "Don't be. You suggested we should cool things off."

She had and she hadn't enjoyed that at all. She thought maybe it would give her some perspective and make her realize that the Candied Apple Café was where her attention needed to be, but instead it had only emphasized how much she missed Mads and Sofia.

"And we have done that. I don't know about you but spending a few days apart hasn't changed anything for me," he said.

She was surprised he'd admitted that and she wanted to tell him it was the same for her. But she wasn't ready to leave herself that vulnerable.

No matter that she'd been very rational when she had decided to not let herself care about Mads. It seemed her heart had a different plan and there was no stopping that.

He looked tired and she wished she hadn't invited her brother over tonight because she'd love to spend the night talking with Mads and baking cookies with Sofia. But this wasn't her family. Hers was coming to her apartment and she had to make things right with her brother.

She just looked at him and realized for the first time that all of the relationships she'd been in that she'd thought she'd been committed to, she hadn't been. Not really. She kept a part of herself safely tucked away. And she only realized it now because she wanted to reach out to Mads but was scared to. She was afraid to take what she wanted from him because she knew he'd lost too much to be able to love like that.

Like she wanted him to.

She simply nodded, then turned to walk away, but he caught her in the hallway. Turned her in his arms and bent to kiss her. It wasn't one of those sweet, soft kisses that promised things would be all right. It was a kiss of desperation and raw need. She put her arms around him and returned it. With the same longing and fear that she'd been trying to pretend she didn't feel. Then she pulled away, stepped back and their eyes met, but neither of them said a word.

She walked away and this time he let her go. She was vaguely aware of getting back to her apartment. She glanced at herself in the mirror, her lipstick was messed up but what caught her attention was that wild look in her eyes. She was on the edge. She hadn't felt like this ever before.

She'd always been so careful to keep her emotions under control. To ensure that she wasn't like her parents, who had one of those relationships where they either didn't talk at all or just fought all the time. But now she understood that bottling up

149

what she felt wasn't the way she wanted to live.

There was a knock on her door and she hesitated. Then used the back of her hand to wipe off the remains of her lipstick before she went and opened the door, forcing a smile on her face.

Nico and Theo waited there. They had flowers and wine and she looked at her brother standing there so nervous.

"Hey, guys. Thank you for coming over despite the short notice."

"We wouldn't miss it," Theo said, handing her the flowers, and he came into the apartment first and brushed his lips against her cheek.

Nico hugged her and then handed her the bottle of wine. "I'm glad. I've missed you both and I want to hear all about your wedding plans."

Chapter 16

Dinner with her brother and Nico was a lot of fun. They told her all about her wedding plans. When Mads and Sofia showed up, Iona had a glimpse of what Christmas morning and every other morning for the rest of her life could be like. And that keen sense of longing she'd been trying to pretend was just a nice-to-have sharpened into a dull ache in her gut. Once again she was forced to admit that she wanted her own family.

"Why did you bring Iona a boat?" Sofia asked as they were all sitting around the living room after dinner, drinking coffee and eating the cookies that the Erikssons had brought.

"Theo's family are in shipping," Iona said. "But isn't there a Greek Christmas tradition involving boats? Sofia is trying to learn about as many of those as she can."

Theo nodded and then smiled at Sofia. "Iona's right, but it's more of a custom than a tradition. This boat that I brought for Iona has something special hidden inside of it."

"It does?" Sofia asked. "Where is it? Can I look for it?"

Iona nodded. She suspected that it would be hidden in the hold of the boat. She went to the table, where the boat was resting, and handed it to Sofia, who held it very carefully, turning it over and they all heard the rattle of something inside.

A smile lit Sofia's face as she started to feel all along the deck of the miniature boat until one of the boards slid open. She reached inside and pulled out a tiny box that had a gold bow on it.

"It's so pretty," Sofia said, bringing it over to Iona.

Iona looked down at the little box, which she knew she wouldn't have found if it wasn't for Sofia. She looked over at Theo.

"Go ahead and open it, Iona."

She opened the box and when she did she saw it held a small charm in the shades of blue of the Turkish Eye. It was a good luck symbol that many Greeks often gifted to newborns. Iona was touched that Nico had given it to her.

"Thank you, Nico."

"You're very welcome. Luck is in no way the same as the gift you gave me when you graciously stepped aside for myself and Theo, but I wanted you to have something special, not only for Christmas but for the rest of your life."

That was one of the sweetest things anyone had ever said to her. "I'm just lucky to see you both so happy."

The charm was on a fine silver chain, which Mads took from her and then put around her neck. She held it for a second and then let it fall back against her body.

"What makes that lucky?" Sofia asked, going over to Theo.

Iona wasn't sure if the little girl wanted one for herself or if she should give the gift to her. But it had clearly been meant for her and Sofia seemed to be aware of that.

"It reflects the evil eye. So, it keeps bad things from happening to the wearer."

"I love it," Sofia said. "What other traditions do you have?"

"Most Greeks are orthodox," Theo said. "So, Nico exchanges gifts on January 1st and not December 25th."

"Really?" Sofia asked. "I bet Remy doesn't know that."

"He might not," Mads said. "You can let the class know in a nice way tomorrow."

"Papa, I'm always nice," Sofia said.

"Except when you're naughty," he retorted.

"It was only that once," Sofia said.

"I can't believe someone as sweet as you could be naughty," Nico said.

"It was a boy at school," Sofia said, still holding the boat and going over to sit on the couch next to Nico.

"Boys always used to get Iona in trouble too," Nico said.

"Did they?" Sofia asked. "Do they still, Iona?"

Iona just laughed. "Sofia inspired our very popular 'naughty and nice' truffles at the Candied Apple Café."

This evening reminded her of how much she loved the holidays and the magic of Christmas. That maybe meeting Mads and starting to become friends and lovers was destined to be, but she had yet to have a good experience with destiny and just riding along with this was harder than she'd expected it to be.

She wanted to smile and enjoy this time. Tonight was absolutely perfect, except there was something deep inside of her that she was afraid of losing. Afraid that this one night would be the closest she'd come to having a family of her own with Mads and Sofia. Not because Mads was insincere or anything like that but because she realized when she'd looked down at the charm that Nico had given her that she didn't believe in luck. She had spent her entire life making her own way and never had she felt like she'd had chance on her side.

Theo and Nico left a short while later and when the door closed behind them she noticed Sofia was still playing with the boat. Mads watched her carefully and she smiled at him, trying to pretend that everything was okay when deep inside she knew it wasn't. She couldn't put her finger on it but something had changed between the two of them.

"Do you want to take the boat home with you?" Iona asked Sofia.

"No, it's yours. I do like it, though," Sofia said.

Mads winked at his daughter. "Go put your shoes on, Sof. It's time for us to go."

"Okay," she said, skipping out of the room.

"Theo and Nico are so good together. Thank you for coming and joining us tonight."

"I wouldn't have missed it," Mads said.

She might be viewing Mads and Sofia in the light that she wanted to see them. And the truth was she had no way of stepping back and being objective. She cared deeply for them. Both of them.

***

"How'd it go last night?" Hayley asked as Iona walked through the kitchen at the Candied Apple the next morning.

Iona touched the charm that had been a gift from Theo. "It turned out really nice. Mads and Sofia brought down some cookies for dessert."

"You guys are getting pretty close," Hayley said.

"I think so. I'm still trying to keep it casual," Iona admitted.

"Good idea," Hayley said.

"Yeah, this is also their first holiday without Gill and I don't want to allow myself to believe that there is something more to it than just friendship."

"I like that in theory, but I've seen the two of you together and there is a definite spark."

"There is." She stopped herself from saying anything else. She'd thought about that night a lot. She had gone over it again and again in her mind. She wondered if Mads had felt he'd let her come too close that night. Shown her his vulnerability in a way he'd never intended.

She had no regrets. She'd always been one of those people who kept looking forward. Even if she knew her actions were dumb she knew she couldn't go back in time and change them

154

and so she'd just stayed focused on making the most of her mistakes. But sleeping with Mads didn't feel like a mistake. Even now she wanted him again.

If he'd said to her that he wanted to keep sleeping together she knew she'd have gone along with it.

But he hadn't. And that left her in this state of not being sure what was happening between the two of them.

"Io?"

"Yeah?"

"Oh, honey, you've got it bad for him, don't you?" Hayley came over to her and put her arm around Iona's shoulders, hugging her close.

"I don't know. I can't see anything clearly with Mads. It's like he's two different people at times. He does things for me that are so sweet and the kind of gesture that strangers don't do for each other and then he doesn't call or text for three or four days. It's so confusing."

"He's a guy. That's how they are. Even being engaged to Garrett hasn't made his motivation any clearer to me," Hayley said. "I mean last night he said he had to work late so I packed us a picnic and brought dinner to him and he was all sweet about it when I was there but when he got home he was different."

Garrett was a cop who'd moved to Internal Affairs right after he and Hayley had gotten engaged. "Maybe something happened that you don't know about."

"Probably. I tried to get him to talk about it but he didn't want to," Hayley said.

"Did you try to force it?" Iona asked.

"Yes. Which is why I was here so early to make the candy. We are definitely ready for the open house and anything else that happens this week."

Iona smiled at her friend. "That is why I'm here early too. I didn't want to stay home and think about last night again. I mean I've rehashed it a million times and tried to figure out if I should have followed him back to his place or just let it alone. It's so hard to figure out if I'm making more mistakes or not."

"I know what you mean. What are you working on this morning?" Hayley asked.

"The final presentation for you and Cici about the offer from the Loughman Group," Iona said. "I think we need to get that wrapped up."

"I know I'm being a control freak but I don't want to do it. What if we can't find someone who will follow my recipes? You know how chefs can be."

"The only one I truly know is you. And you can be a pain about how things are on the palate. So, I imagine that's typical?"

Hayley fake-punched her on the shoulder. "I'm not a pain … well I don't try to be. Part of it is that I don't want our production to become like Dunham Foods. I like that we are unique."

Hayley's family made a famous line of frozen food products and instead of working for the family business she'd struck out on her own to start the Candied Apple.

"I get it. But this is a different type of offer. They want us to be a boutique, niche chocolate shop in each of their hotels. The chocolates in each location will be inspired by the local ingredients."

Hayley sighed. "I would want to go to each location and help design the chocolates."

Which Iona knew wasn't going to happen since Hayley and Garrett were planning a Valentine's Day wedding. "Okay. Let's see what Cici says when she's in the office."

"Okay. Will doing the deal make things better for you and Mads?" Hayley asked.

Iona shook her head. "Our relationship has nothing to do with business."

"Good to know," Hayley said. Her phone pinged and she looked down at it. "Garrett."

Lucy came over from her pillow in the hallway and Iona bent

down to pet the little dog. "Want me to take her out while you call him?"

"Sure. Thanks for letting me vent about Garrett earlier."

"That's what friends are for," Iona said, getting the leash for Lucy and taking her out back. She thought about friendship and knew that she and Mads were laying the groundwork to have a close relationship but she knew that she'd never be happy as just his friend. Yet she had no idea how to tell him that.

She spent the rest of the day at work trying not to think about him but found herself shopping for Christmas presents for both him and Sofia instead of working on the spring marketing plan like she was meant to.

***

Piers flew in on the night of the Candied Apple Café open house so he'd told Sofia they were going to have to miss it. She didn't look too happy with him when he'd explained that Uncle Piers was here for the weekend only.

"He's family, Sof."

"You're right, Papa, but Iona is our friend. And she invited us."

"She'll understand. Remember she had dinner with her brother the other night."

"I know. I just like seeing her."

Mads stopped walking toward Rockefeller Center and pulled Sofia out of the pedestrian traffic. "She likes seeing you too."

Sofia tipped her head back and looked up at him. "Are you sure?"

"Yes. Why is that important to you?"

She looked down at her shoes and shook her head.

"You can tell me."

"It's just nice to have a friend who's a girl," she said at last. "Jessie's my nanny, so she doesn't count."

157

"She'll still be your friend if we miss this open house," Mads said.

She sighed and Mads knew that she wasn't going to give up on this. Iona was important to Sofia. And whatever happened between himself and Iona, he knew that Sofia would want to stay friends with her.

"We can stop by on the way to the Rockettes. Will that work?"

"Yes, Papa. That will be perfect."

"I'm glad. Let me text Uncle Piers and let him know we are running late. Then we need to double back to the Candied Apple," Mads said. He had deliberately made sure they were a block over from the shop even though the walk added extra time to avoid having to go in and see Iona.

It wasn't that he didn't miss her. He did. More than he really wanted to admit, even to himself. It was simply that he was trying to be smart. And seeing Iona made him want to be impulsive. Do things like kiss her or make promises that she wouldn't need to rely on a charm for luck.

Sofia slipped her mittened hand into his as they crossed the street and walked toward the Candied Apple. "I told Remy we were going to be there too."

"Do you like him now?"

She shrugged. "He has been really nice since I saw him with Iona."

"That's the night you were upset. What happened?"

"Nothing. His mommy said that she was glad to see us out this Christmas," Sofia said.

"She said that you?" he asked, surprised. It wasn't the kind of comment that Sofia would be able to understand.

"No. To Remy's dad. But I overheard her," Sofia said. "A lot of adults say things when they think we aren't listening. But Remy heard her too."

"What did he do?"

"He held my hand and said I wasn't naughty at all."

That had been nice of Remy. Mads was beginning to like him. He'd treated Sofia with kindness even when his daughter hadn't been at her best.

"Then why did you cry?" he asked. It sounded to him like Remy's family were caring people.

"I miss Mommy," Sofia said. "I know she can't be here but I wish she was. I think she would have liked Iona too."

Mads tipped his head back and blinked a few times. He knew that his daughter missed Gill. She sometimes told him about it late at night when she woke with a nightmare. And he did think that she and Iona would have gotten on well. And he felt that pang of wishing life had been different for them both.

"I wish she was too," Mads said.

Sofia hugged his legs. "Iona makes me not miss her so much."

"I'm glad," he said, knowing he had to handle whatever was going on with Iona carefully. He didn't want to chance causing Sofia to lose another woman in her life.

There was a line to get into the Candied Apple and he spotted a familiar redhead near the door dressed much the same as she'd been the first day they'd met. She had on that short red velvet dress trimmed in white faux fur. Her legs looked longer than ever and the bell on the top of her Santa hat jingled as she turned her head towards them.

She waved at them and Sofia ran over to talk to her. Mads stayed back. He was not handling this very well. He'd promised himself he'd protect Sofia from more heartache and he'd never guessed that he could be the cause of it. That his feelings for Iona might make him let her close to his daughter and then he'd have to be the one to deal with things if he and Iona didn't work out.

And how could they? He wasn't ready for someone else in his life. He'd promised himself he'd never fall in love again. Never care so deeply for another person save Sofia that he'd be broken if they died. He couldn't do it again.

"Come on, Papa. We don't have to wait on the line," Sofia said as she came back and took his hand, leading him towards the store.

Iona smiled as they approached and waved them in. "Thank you for stopping by."

He noticed she had on her lucky charm necklace and wondered if it would protect her from him and his frozen heart.

"No problem. We can't stay long. We're on our way to Radio City Music Hall."

"It's just nice to see you both," she said. "Don't forget to pick up your 'naughty and nice' truffles."

"We won't," Sofia said.

When he went by her, Iona squeezed his hand and smiled at him in a way that was sweet and personal. More intimate than the smile she flashed at the crowd. Or maybe that was just because he realized how much he liked her and wished that he was a different kind of man so he could claim her for himself.

Chapter 17

The Christmas markets at Bryant Park had always been one of Iona's favorite things to see during the holiday season. The fact that she was by herself this year tinged her shopping trip with a little longing. She and Theo usually came down here and picked out tchotchkes for their mom, but Nico had invited him to go to the Hamptons to meet his family this weekend so she was on her own. She loved the painted wooden ornaments that were sold in one of the booths.

It was a clear and cool Saturday morning and the market was busy. Iona had tried to go help out at the Candied Apple, but they had more staff than needed on hand and she had been getting in the way. So here she was. Shopping by herself and wishing she'd said yes when Hayley had asked if she wanted to go to Boston with her this weekend.

"Hi Iona!" Sofia said excitedly, coming up next to her. "Papa, it's Iona. I knew it had to be you."

Iona glanced over at Mads, who was a few feet from his daughter. His coat was open, revealing a black sweater over his jeans and loafers. Sofia had a stocking cap on her head and her red coat was still buttoned up.

"Hi there. Are you shopping for anything in particular?"

"I need a present for Miss Pembroke," Sofia said. "And Papa is supposed to help me find something for Secret Santa."

"I love Secret Santa. Who did you get?"

"Jennifer. She's pretty nice. I am hoping to find a ballerina ornament for her," Sofia said.

"You're in luck," Iona said. "I saw one over at that booth."

She pointed to the one she'd been at a few minutes earlier.

"Want to come with me to pick it out?" Sofia asked.

Iona glanced over at Mads and he nodded subtly. "I'd love to. I usually get my mom some version of Santa for her tree. I know he's not your thing, but maybe you can help me pick out a different ornament for her."

"I will. Is that a tradition for you?" Sofia asked.

"Sofia, don't be nosey," Mads interrupted.

"I don't mind," Iona said. "Yes, it is. Usually, Theo is here to help me but he couldn't come today. On Christmas Eve we sneak it onto our mom's place setting at the dinner table."

"Does she know it's from you two?" Sofia asked.

Iona smiled down at her. "She always pretends she doesn't know. When Nico and I were little we loved the thought of surprising her."

"That sounds like a fun idea," Sofia said. Then she tugged on Iona's hand until she bent down and she leaned in close to her. "Maybe you can help me do that for Papa?"

"I would love to," Iona said.

When they got to the booth, Sofia let go of Iona's hand and stood on tiptoe to look at all of the ornaments. There were three ballerinas on the wooden pegs near the back of the booth and Mads gestured for her and Sofia to go first.

She followed the little girl, who was very careful in her selection, looking carefully at every brunette ballerina on the peg before making her choice.

Sofia waited until Mads wasn't close enough and then pointed to a Christmas tree that had a man holding a little girl on his shoulders to put the angel on the top of the tree. "Can you get that one for Papa?" she asked.

"I can."

As she stood up, Iona noticed a wooden knight on a peg behind the cash register that reminded her of the book that Iona had read to her.

Mads paid for Sofia's purchase while Sofia spotted a friend from school and went over to talk to her.

"Did you find anything?" Mads asked her.

"I did. I'll be right out if you want to go with Sofia."

"Thank you for sharing your ornament tradition with Sof," Mads said, with that bit of sadness in his eyes. He had to be thinking of Gill again. "We will be out front when you're done."

He turned away and she watched him go. She didn't know how he handled it. How hard it must be for Mads to do all these things without the woman he loved.

She purchased the ornament she'd seen for Sofia and the one that Sofia wanted for her father, asking for them to be wrapped separately before tucking them both into her handbag before she went outside. They spent the rest of the afternoon shopping. Sofia found a present for her teacher; Iona found a couple of treats for Hayley's dog, Lucy. Sofia wanted to buy something for the dog as well and picked out a scarf that had dogs wearing Santa hats on it. It was cute and she could tell by how much Sofia talked about it that the little girl wanted a dog too.

"We've already discussed this, Sof. No dogs. We do have time to go and see the gingerbread village at the Common, do you want to join us, Iona?"

"Please, Iona, please! Papa is taking me for tea afterward. With cookies and little sandwiches."

"That sounds perfect," Iona said. Though a part of her felt like she should say no, she went with them. Anything was better than heading back to her empty apartment and wishing for something that wasn't hers.

"It's an Ugly Sweater Party," Iona said on the phone. "I think that Sofia will enjoy it. If you guys can make it, stop by around six."

"We don't have any ugly sweaters," Mads said.

"I've seen some of your sweaters so I'd have to agree.

I left a couple for you with the doorman," Iona said. "I have this party every year and my mom is going to be there and Theo and Nico. Anyway I'd love it if you could come. We also watch *Rudolph the Red Nosed Reindeer* and sort of shout advice at the characters and of course sing along to all the songs."

He hadn't watched a Christmas television show in years. Gill had preferred to keep the holidays about religion, so while they'd seen different versions of *The Nativity* and *The Little Drummer Boy*, he hadn't seen Rudolph since he and Piers had been ten and eleven.

"I don't think Sofia will know the show."

"Are you kidding me? Then she'll love this. It's a lot of fun. And last year, Cici's brothers dressed like Hermey the dentist elf from *Rudolph and the Head Elf*. They were hilarious, arguing with each other all night. You don't have to come but I'd love to see you both. I really enjoyed tea with you guys the other day and now I'd like to share some of my holiday traditions with you."

He knew he couldn't turn her down. If Sofia heard about it she'd be upset with him.

"Okay, we will stop by. Can Jessie come? It sounds like her kind of thing," Mads said.

"Yes. I like Jessie. She's brought Sofia by the shop a few times after school," Iona said.

"I didn't know about that."

"I don't think it was meant to be a secret," Iona said. "But I didn't mean to speak out of turn."

Mads shook his head, even though she couldn't see him. "I'm

164

not going to yell at them for stopping by to see you."

"That's good to know," Iona said with a little laugh. "Also, I usually just make a huge pot of chili for dinner. Can Sofia eat that?"

"She loves it."

"Perfect. I'll see you both later then," Iona said, hanging up the phone.

Mads sat back in his chair and thought about how busy they'd been this Christmas season. They had plans to go ice skating the following afternoon with Remy from Sofia's class. He knew that he'd wanted this year to be different but he wondered if he was filling the time with too many activities. He tried talking to his daughter, but frankly the words sometimes escaped him. He had no idea how to find out if she was doing okay. If he was helping her through this first Christmas without Gill the right way or if he was doing it wrong.

He hoped that he was doing it right. He checked his schedule and saw that he didn't have any meetings until the end of the day and decided he'd leave early and go meet Sofia after school. He texted Jessie that he'd pick her up and about the party at Iona's.

He had his driver drop him off in front of the Lycée Francaise, where Sofia went to school and stood to one side as the kids exited the building. He saw Sofia wearing her uniform, carrying something in one hand.

"Sofia."

"Papa, I didn't know you were coming to pick me up today," she said, coming over to him, hugging him.

"I hope you don't mind."

"I don't. Look what I made today at school."

"What is it?" he asked, holding a picture up that she'd drawn. It looked like a cylinder with three matches on it.

"It's a yule log. Did you know that the period leading up to Christmas is a festival of light?"

"I'd heard something about that," he said. "Is this meant to be a log?"

"Yes. I ran out of time to color it," she said. "Miss Pembroke sent home instructions if we want to make one for ourselves."

He took her hand and led the way to their car, which was parked at the end of the block. "Do we want to?"

She smiled up at him. He noticed one of her front teeth was a little bit loose. She was going to lose a tooth. It was one of the things that Gill had mentioned she'd never get to see and Mads' heart hurt.

"I do, Papa."

He nodded and Sofia kept on talking, but he was thinking of all the things that Gill had missed and how much he missed her. They got in the car and Hamlisch drove them back to their building on the Upper East Side. The doorman was waiting for them when they walked through the lobby.

"Hi Greg," Sofia said. "Want to see a picture I drew at school today?"

The doorman nodded. "I do."

She showed him the drawing and he complimented her on it. "I have something for you too."

"You do?" Sofia asked. "What is it?"

"I don't know. I think it's from St. Nick."

"He's not a real person," Sofia said. "Who really dropped it off?"

The doorman looked over Sofia's head at him. Mads reached around to take the gaily wrapped packages from him. "It's from Iona."

"Oh, that's nice. We don't have anything for her, do we?" Sofia asked.

"She's invited us to an Ugly Sweater Party," Mads said. "She even provided sweaters for us."

"When is it?"

"Tonight. Do you want to go?"

"Yes, Papa. I do. Do you think it will be fun? I wonder how ugly our sweaters will be."

Sofia chatted all the way up to their floor and when they entered their apartment Jessie was in the kitchen with Sofia's after-school snack. Mads left her to go down to his bedroom. He sat down on the edge of his bed. Then fell back, staring at the ceiling. He missed Gill. He hated that her illness had stolen these moments from her. She would have loved seeing Sofia as she was growing up. Becoming her own little person and yet at times more like him and then even more like Gill.

**

Iona was in her bedroom, fixing her lipstick. She heard the voices and the laughter from the rest of her apartment. Theo and Nico had arrived wearing matching sweaters. They looked very cute. Her mom had brought her dog Fifi. Valentina had on a sweater with Fifi's picture and Fifi was wearing one with Valentina's. It had cracked Iona up when she saw it.

It had also made her a little sad that her father had never appreciated her mom. She made everything so much fun with things like the sweaters, which her dad would have seen as a waste of money.

But Mads and Sofia hadn't shown up and everyone had someone special here for them but her.

There was a knock on her door and she glanced up to find her mom in the doorway.

"Just checking on you," Valentina said as she entered the room.

"I'm fixing my lipstick."

"Uh huh, seems like you're hiding out."

"Mads didn't show up," she said to her mom. "I don't know if I'm really meant to do this relationship thing. I mean at work it's … hard but easier than this. I know how to achieve the result I want."

167

Her mom laughed and came over to stand next to her, adjusting Iona's hair behind her ear. "Darling, that's the way life is. It's not meant to be easy. And you've achieved more than enough at work."

"Dad wouldn't have thought so," she said.

"Your dad would never say it to you, but he was proud of you. He thought you'd one day take over his position as CEO. He said you were hungrier than Theo."

Tears burned her eyes. Her father's words touched her. "Thanks, Mom."

"Also don't worry about Mads not being here. Children aren't the best helpers to being on time."

"You're right," she said.

"Let's get back to the party," Valentina said, taking Iona's arm and leading her out of the room.

She mingled and directed her guests to the kitchen buffet for food and she was watching everyone dish up their bowls of chili when she'd realized that this was her life. She was so blessed in her family and friends. Too bad her father hadn't let anyone close to him in this way.

The doorbell rang and Iona assumed it was Hayley, Garrett, and Lucy. Hayley had texted her earlier to say they were running late because Garrett had been hung up by something at work.

She opened the door to find Mads and Sofia standing there.

"Hello you two, I thought you might have had a conflict," she said.

He shook his head and was smiling. "We didn't."

"I love my sweater, Iona. I know it's supposed to be ugly but I love it," Sofia said as she came around from behind her dad. The sweater was ballerinas wearing Darth Vader helmets. She'd seen it online and she knew that Sofia would like it.

"I thought you would," she said. She didn't bother trying to convince the little girl that the gift had been from St. Nick. She knew better.

Sofia came further into the room. Mads wore the sweater she'd bought for him: a red and green nylon one that said BAH HUMBUG on it.

"Thanks for this. I might wear it to work tomorrow," he said.

"Ha. I know you won't. Where is Jessie?" Iona asked.

"Her boyfriend invited her to go ice skating so I gave her the evening off."

"Sounds like fun," Iona said. "Are you hungry?"

"Yes," Mads said. "We are, aren't we, Sof?"

"Yup. Papa wouldn't let me eat anything before we came down here."

"Were you hungry? I said no to the bag of candy the neighbors dropped off. You could have had an apple."

"I wasn't hungry for an apple," Sofia said. "But for chocolate."

"I don't have any chocolate but I do have chili," Iona said.

Iona led the way into the kitchen and got them bowls of chili and then led them into the living room. Hayley and Garrett arrived a few minutes later, they wore matching sweaters with a dachshund on them and for Lucy they had a dog sweater with stick figures of a man and woman holding hands. Lucy and Fifi both got along well and soon were sitting on the floor near the fireplace.

Iona laughed when she saw it. After everyone finished eating they went into the living room to start watching "Rudolph" with everyone laughing and singing along. Iona realized as Sofia climbed on her lap to watch the movie she'd been given a real gift when she met these two.

They were turning into the kind of friends that she could count on and she felt so blessed to have them in her life. She felt a hand on her shoulder and looked up to see Theo standing there.

He didn't say anything, just squeezed her shoulder and she reached up to clench his hand. "I'm glad you two are here tonight."

"Me too. I've missed you."

She had missed him too but she couldn't say that because her throat felt heavy with tears. She wanted to say they were happy tears or to blame it on her period but she knew she was overcome with emotion because everything was changing and she still felt, despite her new friends, that she'd stayed the same. That she was still the same woman she'd been at the beginning of the year.

Like everyone else had figured out life and she'd been left behind. And that wasn't true. Nico leaned down and kissed her forehead before moving back over to Theo. And Iona turned her attention back to the movie but she wasn't really paying attention to it.

Sofia's head fell to her shoulder and she looked up at Iona. "The reindeer aren't very nice."

"No, they aren't. Definitely on the naughty list," Iona said after clearing her throat.

"But I wouldn't run away," Sofia said. "That's not the solution."

"It's not?" Iona asked, happy to have this distraction from her own problems.

"No. Papa always says if you leave a mess it will be there when you come back."

"Your papa is very smart," Iona said.

"He is. But he leaves a mess in the bathroom."

"He does?" she asked, curious as to what kind of mess he left. It was interesting to think she'd slept with him but didn't really know him as well as she thought she did.

"Yes. He leaves his towel in a pile on the floor."

"Are you telling secrets on me, Sof?"

"I just wanted to make sure Iona knows you can be naughty sometimes too," Sofia said.

Iona laughed and Mads just shook his head. "This is the thanks I get for letting her stay up late."

"You're welcome, Papa," she said, scooting over to sit between her and Mads. Sofia took both of their hands in hers and Iona

170

just held the little girl's hand and watched the movie, pretending that nothing had changed. But she knew that everything had.

Chapter 18

The fire crackled. The smell of the wood burning and the mellow feel produced by the brandy made it seem like all of Iona's problems were worlds away. It had been a few days since her party and she had decided to stop pretending she didn't want to make their relationship more solid, but still he was hesitating. Realistically, she knew it was past time for her to go back to her own apartment. She had a big promotion kicking off tomorrow morning that she wanted to be in store to oversee. But she didn't want to leave.

She'd been encouraging Sofia to make a list for Christmas by telling her she could give it to her father and not Santa. Tonight she'd shown Iona a few of the items on there and asked what she wanted for Christmas.

Iona had always been one of those girls who took the time to make a Christmas list. To write down all the things she wanted and then being spoiled by her parents when it came to material things. She'd usually get them all. The first time she realized that Santa wasn't real she'd been almost thirteen. She'd heard the stories at school and had stopped talking about the jolly man in the red suit to her friends, but somehow Santa had always delivered for her. Until that one Christmas when she'd waited for something money couldn't buy. She'd craved just a little praise from her father and had asked for it each night in December as she'd looked to the North Star, whispering her wish. And on Christmas morning she'd had her usual pile of presents and nothing had changed with her father.

It had been sobering.

"More brandy?" Mads asked, returning to the living room. He still wore the thick gray cable-knit mock turtleneck sweater that made his blue-grey eyes even icier.

She shook her head. "No thanks."

He poured two fingers into his own snifter and then sat down next to her. "You look very serious staring into the fire."

"I was thinking about Sofia and Santa and remembering when I stopped believing."

He stretched his long legs out in front of him, propping them on a leather hassock under the coffee table as his hand fell to her shoulder.

"When was that?"

"Sixteen."

"Surely you stopped before then."

"I had heard the stories at school but Christmas at my house is huge. And Santa never disappointed. *Never*," she said, taking another sip.

"So, what happened?"

"I wanted something money couldn't buy," she admitted. "Something that couldn't be delivered by Macy's."

"What was it?"

"My dad to be proud of me," she said.

"Ah, I see ... actually how did you think that would work?" he asked gently.

"I had been given an opportunity at school to attend the mock UN in DC and they only select a small number of kids in the entire US. I waited until Christmas morning to tell him. I had it all planned out in my head, how he would react and everything.

I knew that Santa and the general Christmas magic would influence him and for this one morning I'd catch a glimpse of pride or maybe he'd even actually say, "good job".

"But that didn't happen. I followed him around all day waiting for some sort of Christmas miracle and nothing. Finally, he just told me to go and take the new car he'd gotten me for a spin," she admitted.

He put his hand on her thigh and squeezed it softly, comfortingly.

"I never tried to ask for anything from God or the universe until Gill got sick. I prayed every night that the new drug would work. Not because I'd ever been deeply faithful but because I needed to believe that miracles could happen. And I'm not going to lie, a little bit of me wanted to believe what I saw in advertising and in holiday movies. That this really was the season of miracles. That Gill was going to beat her cancer and everything would go back to the way it was."

She had no words listening to him. Hearing the gut- wrenching pain in his voice, she turned to him and saw him staring into the flames, watching them leap and dance. But Iona knew that Mads saw something else. He was seeing Gill and reliving her illness. "Tomorrow will be the day that we started to know the end was near. One year since she started to get really bad and the hospice nurse upped her dosage. I just can't let go of the anger I feel. I went to church and raged at the priest. My mom had been sending me the Footprints in the Sand, psalm 77 print for years. Telling me that God would carry me when I needed him and instead I realized there were only one set of footprints because I was alone … well I had Sofia, who I was carrying."

He didn't say anything else and she took a deep breath. He was broken. But she'd known that from the moment they'd met in the elevator. When they'd become reluctant friends because they were both down on their luck, but unlike her who was taking a temporary hit, it seemed that Mads was down for the count.

How could she help him?

His faith in God and his relationship there was one he'd have to come back to on his own. She knew if she said that God sometimes delivered what was needed instead of wanted, she would drive a wedge between them that would never be budged.

"Why do you think they call it the season of miracles?" she asked instead.

"I'm not sure what that means. I don't think I've ever seen one."

He turned to face her. She saw the glint of tears in his eyes and knew talking about miracles wasn't going to help him tonight.

"Oh, Mads," she said. "Sofia is your miracle. She's finding new traditions for you and making this Christmas special."

"She is. I'm so blessed to have her. I was afraid when Gill was first diagnosed that I wouldn't be able to raise Sofia on my own. I suggested we ask her grandparents to raise her, but Gill … she had a temper when she got mad and that really ticked her off.

"She told me to stop feeling sorry for myself. That Sofia was going to be the best daughter in the world because she was part of her and me," Mads said, his voice going quiet at the end.

Gill was wise. How hard it must have been for her to watch her husband and daughter as she slipped away from them. It made Iona want to cry.

"Do we want a good cry or do we need a laugh?" she asked after a few moments.

"Men don't cry," he said.

"That's so last century," she quipped back.

"Agree, but if I start, Io, I might never stop," he said with a seriousness that just made her want to cry for him.

But that wasn't going to help. She knew that miracles weren't real. That she wasn't going to magically transform his Christmas, but their friendship was real. And she did know how to make people laugh.

"Dance off."

"What?"

"Sofia told me you had some moves back in the day and showed me a video of you boogie-ing with your brother."

"We were drunk," Mads said.

"You have natural rhythm."

"You took ballet until you were fifteen," he said. "I don't think I can beat you."

"Good."

"I thought you were going to let me win," he said.

"Why ever did you think that? We both are competitive."

He nodded. "Okay, then, I'm not going to make it easy on you."

"Fair enough."

***

Mads was on the cusp of losing it. Really losing it. He knew it and he could tell that Iona did too. But as she turned to Alexa and asked the machine to play dance music, the first song to come up was the "Macarena". She looked at him, with one eyebrow raised.

"I was the champ at school to this song," she said. She got to her feet, shaking her hips to the music. "I'll go first."

She did a slow circle and then instead of doing the common line-dance moves did her own combination of salsa moves, which were distracting him. Making him forget about the holidays, this wretched *first* that was hanging around his soul like a lead anchor. Iona filled the room as she always did with her sunny personality and her sensuality.

She had a pair of skin-tight jeans that clung to her long legs and a sweater that was loose fitting but did nothing to disguise the shape of her body. With each sensuous shake of her hips, he forgot a little more and just heard the music. And despite the fact that they were on the Upper East Side, with snow and ice outside, he felt transported to Cuba.

He stood there watching until she threw her hand out towards him.

"Your turn."

His turn? *His turn.* They were having a dance-off.

He wasn't really much of a dancer unless he'd been drinking, and drinking a lot, so his moves pretty much were limited to putting his hands on his hips and making a circle with them. She threw her head back and started laughing.

"What, you don't like this?" he asked, shimmying his way over to her. He danced around her, clapping to the music and then he put her hand on his hip. "That's fear, right? I noticed your moves weren't quite as good as mine, but since I'm a gentleman I'll show you how it's done."

She glanced over her shoulder at him, their eyes met and she smiled. "I can't wait to see what you have to teach me."

"You will be impressed."

She laughed and then he spun her around to face him, putting one hand on her waist and taking her right hand in his. He pulled her close to him and her curves fit nicely against his body. The sensation overwhelming him for a moment and he realized how much he'd missed touching someone. Not sex. He'd gone out and done that with a bar hook-up over the summer just to have it out of the way. But touching and intimacy.

Their eyes met, her lips were parted, and she gently took her hand from his and brought both up to wrap behind his neck. She went up on tiptoe and their lips brushed. He could tell from the way she did it that she meant the embrace to be a casual one. Nothing too hot and heavy but a spark arched between them, burning him straight to his core. Making him forget things that he'd thought he never would and he put his hand in her hair at the back of her neck, kissing her with all the passion he'd thought he'd never feel again. She tipped her head to the side as he deepened the kiss.

His hands rubbed the column of her neck, her fingers soft and long and everything narrowed down to Iona. The way her lush lips parted under his. The taste of brandy on her tongue and the way her height made it easier to hold her. His hand on her waist drifted lower, cupping her backside and drawing her into the curve of his body.

The music changed but he didn't register it. The dance-off had been a distraction and he'd thought it had been from the past, but he stepped back, looking down into Iona's upturned face, her lips were parted and swollen slightly from his kisses. Her skin was flushed and her eyes half-closed and he had to admit that the sadness he'd felt was because she was fresh and new to love and he wanted to be the kind of man who could believe in miracles and forever because he knew if he'd met her before Gill, he would have wanted that with her.

Not that he hadn't loved his wife. He had. Oh, God. *Had he loved her.*

He turned away from Iona and walked out of the room.

What was he thinking? She'd died and now he was holding another woman, wishing he still believed in love because … he liked Iona. It wasn't just lust or loneliness. He truly liked her with her quirky sense of humor and her willingness to do anything for a friend.

He heard sounds of her moving around behind him and a moment later she was next to him. "I think I'm going to go. Thanks for a fun evening."

"Don't. Please don't leave."

She tipped her head to the side and shook it. "I can't stay. I want something that you're not ready for. And I'm trying to be a good friend to you, Mads. You need a friend and so does Sofia."

It was as he'd thought. Not fair to Iona to ask her for more when he wasn't the man she deserved. And if he needed further proof that there wasn't a higher being watching out for him, he'd just gotten it. Why would God put her in his path now? Why would he give him this woman, who could be so much more if only he hadn't been so badly shattered by Gill's death?

"Fair enough. Text me when you're back to your place."

"It's not that far," she said. "I think I'll be safe."

"I'll worry if you don't," he said.

She started to say something but then just shook her head. "Okay."

"What were you going to say?"

"Nothing that matters," she said. "Don't forget the gingerbread decorating tomorrow at Sofia's school. I brought some candies over for her to take in. They are on the counter in a Candied Apple Café bag."

She had become a part of their lives and he realized that as he nodded at her and watched her walk down the hall. That he had to stop taking from her. He either had to find a way to give her what she deserved from him or just let her go.

***

Lucy was curled up next to the fireplace and when Iona entered she came over to greet her; she was watching the little dog while Hayley and Garrett were in Boston for an overnight trip. Iona sank to the floor and let the little dog climb up on her lap. Lucy put her paws in the middle of Iona's chest and then licked her chin as Iona lowered her head.

She'd spent hours thinking of herself as a fixer. She knew that her super power — if she had one — was down to the fact that she'd always been able to see the broken things in others and fix them. Even without a degree in psychology she knew that it owed a lot to the fact that she'd rather analyze others and figure out what motivated them. That had always been the secret to her success at all of her jobs.

She took comfort from cuddling the tiny miniature dachshund.

She was grown and she knew there was no such thing as a Christmas miracle. She'd paid lip service to that sentiment earlier, but tonight she realized it was true. The part of her that had always been able to tap into the joy of the holiday season felt small and gray. She looked around her apartment, decorated with garlands and twinkling with lights. She waited for the holiday things to cheer her up but she finally understood the lyrics from "Blue Christmas". Finally she knew that missing one person could cut deep. And the worst part was Mads missed Gill and Iona thought she missed Mads.

Lucy gave her one last lick and then trotted back to her bed and Iona stayed there on the floor taking off her boots and then pulling her legs up to her chest. She hadn't allowed her belief in the holidays to be shaken until tonight.

Maybe she was tired.

Yeah, that was it.

But as she forced herself to her feet, she knew it wasn't fatigue. Or not the normal kind. It was a kind of soul wariness that had been spawned by nothing more than a desire for once to have someone for herself. Someone who could mend the broken bits inside of her.

And, of course, her heart wanted a man who was so far from being healed no matter what he'd said. Mads was going to take years to heal from the blow of his wife's death. And she got that because she was coming to love him and little Sofia. Iona knew that it wasn't that crazy lust-driven emotion that she'd sometimes called love while in the flush of a new relationship. It was some-thing deeper.

Something more profound.

And that was what frightened her. She went into the kitchen and made herself a cup of hot cocoa from the new Candied Apple at Home line. And then took it up to her loft bedroom. She set it on the dresser and then fiddled with her iPhone dock until her Christmas playlist came on. She did her bedtime ritual, thinking too much about things she couldn't have.

But the truth was she'd always been hungry for something but had never really known what. And there was no easy answer. She climbed into bed as her phone pinged and she reached for it to see it was a text from Mads.

White Christmas is playing on TCM.

Iona sighed. She should probably ignore the text. But he'd reached out to her. She knew then that this was the part of complicated she couldn't plan for or anticipate. He wanted her but he was still tangled in the briars of the past. She needed this tentative olive branch he'd offered her.

Iona replied. *It's one of my favorites.*

Mine too. Sorry for … just sorry, pinged back.

Me too.

She wanted to say more but didn't know what, so instead she watched the movie and laughed when Mads texted her about asking his brother to try the fan dance when he saw him on Christmas Day.

She texted back that she thought Mads had nice calves, so the act sounded promising.

They continued texting until the movie ended with that miracle snowfall that saved the ski season and Rosemary Clooney and Bing Crosby reconciled.

She wished life was that easy. That the miracle she sought would just appear like a snowstorm.

Iona texted one last time: *Night.*

Mads replied. *I'm going to try to count my blessings tonight.*

She just sent back a smiley face. She knew he was trying and the thing she had to decide was if she was going to continue to try or if she was going to just let the burgeoning feelings she had for him fall to the side.

Chapter 19

The Common lobby looked like a lavish Christmas card: the staff were dressed in Victorian period costumes and there was a string quartet in the corner of the lobby playing carols. Iona stopped in the doorway just to take this all in. It was hard for her to believe that Mads had put this all together.

He wasn't a Scrooge, exactly, but the traditions of the holidays weren't where his mind normally went. And this was like the most perfect Christmas dream come to life.

He came over to her, looking like a million dollars in his dinner jacket and tie. He was a handsome man, something she'd been reminded of each night when she went to sleep and woke to sensual dreams of him. She'd tried to pull back to keep them both from being swept up in the magic of the season but a part of her knew that it was too late.

"Let me take your coat," he said. She turned so he could help her remove her long red wool coat.

She felt the brush of his breath against her bare neck as he pulled the coat from her arms. The Common holiday party was formal so she wore a strapless, floor-length black velvet gown. She'd decided that her red satin elbow-length gloves were the perfect accent and had worn her grandmother's stacked pearl choker at her neck. She'd put her hair up in a chignon and she was happy with the way she looked tonight.

And when she turned around and saw the look in Mads' eyes she knew he was too. And that feeling of longing that had been driving her for too long felt as if it might be close to finding someone to satisfy it.

He put his hand on the small of her back as he escorted her across the lobby. She was aware of the people who looked at them as they walked and she knew they looked like they belonged together. In her heart, she'd already started to see them both as a couple. He was tall, dark, and so handsome he took her breath away when she thought of him. They fit together perfectly and she was tired of pretending they didn't.

He handed her coat over at the coat check and then led her down a long hallway, which she recalled led to the banquet rooms.

Mads pulled her to a stop in one of the conversation alcoves. She glanced up at him, their eyes meeting, and he opened his mouth to say something but stopped before he uttered a word.

"What is it?"

"I told myself that I'd never feel this way about another woman. I've been living in a sort of chrysalis state, pretending that I didn't need anything except Sofia, but now you are making me realize how lonely and empty I've been."

"I am?" she asked. She lifted her hand to touch the side of his face, knowing how hard that had to be for him to admit.

He didn't say anything, only leaned in to kiss her and in that brush of his lips against hers she felt all the words he couldn't say. When she pulled back she saw a light in his eyes that hadn't been there before and believed that he was starting to fall for her. The way she'd fallen for him.

"Mads …"

"Sir, sorry to interrupt but you're needed in the ballroom," Lexi said, coming over to join them.

Mads' assistant was dressed in a green cocktail dress and gave Iona an apologetic look.

"It's okay," he said. "Just had to steal a kiss before we got to the party, where I'll be too busy to even dance with Iona."

"I don't blame you," Lexi said. "And I added the first dance to your agenda so you'd get one with her."

"Thank you, Lexi," Mads said and his assistant walked away. He turned to Iona. "I'm sorry, but tonight I'll be working as much as attending the party."

"It's fine," she said. This was what his life was. The Common took a lot of his time and she understood that.

They went down the hall to the ballroom that was set up with tables spread out around a dance floor. There was a stage at one end and then three open bars dotted around the room. There were round tables that could each seat ten people and a seating chart was mounted near the door when they came in.

In one corner was a Christmas tree that stretched to the ceiling and was lit with brightly colored strands of lights. Iona stood for a moment, just taking in the room, which was festive and crowded with a good number of people.

"Lexi, where am I supposed to be?" he asked his assistant, but he kept his hand on Iona's back.

"The board have all arrived. You need to go and greet them and then we need a picture of all of you. For the electronic Christmas card I'm sending out tomorrow."

"I'll wait over here," Iona said.

"No. Come with me," Mads said. "The board members always bring their spouses. I'd like for you to meet them."

"Even though we turned down your offer to work with you?" she asked.

"Yes. That was just business," he said. "Plus, I think you might change your mind once Hayley has a chance to talk to some of the other chefs I'm flying in to meet her."

Interesting. He saw her refusal as just the first stage in negotiating. She tucked that away for later. Iona didn't share Mads' opinion on that. But she did hope that Hayley would loosen up her control over their product. The decision to not take the Loughman Group up on their offer had been a difficult one for the three of them to make.

"Okay, then I will go with you."

He didn't say anything else, just led her over to the board members and when he introduced her she noticed that many of the board looked at her with speculation in their eyes and she knew that was because this was another first for Mads. His first time at a corporate function with someone other than Gill.

***

"It's good to see you dating," Derek Martin, the CFO of the Loughman Group said when they were at the bar getting refills for Iona and Derek's wife Marcia.

Mads looked back at Iona where she was talking with Marcia and two of the other spouses. She had fit into the group at their table very well. But that hadn't surprised him. She was social and entertaining and he'd yet to see her in a situation where she couldn't handle herself and win over the people around her.

"Thanks," Mads said.

"How is Sofia?" Derek asked.

"She's been good," Mads replied, not really wanting to talk too much about his daughter. But Derek was more of a friend than just a colleague. "Most days she's good. But every once in a while, she has a meltdown."

"That's to be expected."

Derek and he had started at the Loughman Group together more than ten years ago, so Derek had known Gill before she got sick.

"Yes, it is."

"You know that I'm here if you need me. Any time of the day or night."

"I do know," Mads said. "Thank you."

"I still miss Gill," Derek said.

"I do too," Mads said. "But it doesn't hurt the way it used to."

Derek clapped him on the shoulder.

Mads wasn't really ready to admit that he'd started moving on, but he knew he had. Bringing Iona tonight had been his first step forward out of the past with Gill. And he didn't feel the guilt like he had in the past when he'd thought of this moment. He hadn't brought a woman to a work party in years. Of course, when Gill was sick no one had expected him to, but at the summer picnic he'd had some well-meaning employees and fellow Loughman Group board members introducing him to their single friends.

The bartender finished making Derek's drinks and his friend collected them and stepped aside while Mads ordered a Manhattan for himself and Iona. He was vaguely aware of Derek talking to one of the front desk managers, but his mind was on what his friend had said.

He'd been trying to be careful. Just experience as many of these last firsts without Gill and not lose his sanity. But somewhere along the way Iona had become the focus of the firsts. They were no longer "withouts" but "withs". He knew that deep inside and with that knowledge came more fear than he wanted to admit he could feel. He was afraid of letting himself care for Iona in this way.

Afraid that something would happen to her.

The last time he'd felt this kind of anticipation and hope had been when Sofia was born and then shortly after that Gill had gotten sick. He'd never just been able to let himself fully love without feeling like there was a price to pay.

He took their drinks back to the table and Iona looked up at him with a question in her eyes, but he just shook his head.

Tonight had felt like a step forward but now the ghosts of the past were holding on to him and they weren't letting go.

He had seen her with her friends and her mom and brother and knew that Iona needed a family of her own. He could feel how ready she was to create her own little unit because she spent a lot of time working and he knew that was what he had used to fill his time when he'd been trying to avoid his home life.

But now he knew that his fear was going to play a part in this. Was probably going to keep him from giving her his heart.

And was that fair?

But then he remembered what Piers had said when Mads had gotten drunk after first learning that Gill was terminal. *Who said life was meant to be fair?*

Really. Who had? He knew it wasn't. But he wasn't too sure that Iona was going to want to spend the rest of her life with a man who would only let her into his bed and could only offer her affection and nothing more.

He also realized he couldn't ask her to do that. Because he wanted more for her. He wanted her to find that kind of deep and abiding love that he'd shared with Gill. That love that had dominated every aspect of their life until her illness had taken over.

And he knew then that the only gift he could give her this Christmas was to let her go. To let her find someone who she could build the family she craved with.

She tipped her head to the side, giving him a quizzical look, but he couldn't say anything, not right now.

"Dance with me," he said, holding out his hand.

The DJ was playing a version of *Baby, It's Cold Outside* with Idina Menzel and Michael Bublé. She took his hand and he led her to the dance floor, pulling her into his arms and swinging her around.

She placed one hand on his shoulder and he held her other one.

"Are you okay?" she asked.

"As okay as I can be," he admitted.

She started to say something else but he just put his mouth over hers as much to taste her kiss again as to stem the questions he didn't want to answer. He was taking this night for himself. To tuck away with the other memories that he used to keep himself company on the long lonely nights. This night and then he'd let her go. Let her go back to her life and her Christmassy spirit of joy and hopefulness.

The song changed to the *Christmas Waltz* and he was grateful to hold her for a few more seconds. The rest of the evening went by too quickly and since Jessie wasn't expecting him until morning he felt greedy when he asked her to join him in the Presidential Suite for the rest of the evening.

"I'd love to."

***

Iona was buzzing from the Manhattans she'd drunk and from dancing with Mads. She could tell that something was bothering him, but each time she tried to talk to him he'd pulled her into his arms or distracted her with something. *But now they were alone.*

The Presidential Suite was large and luxurious. Bigger than some apartments, she'd imagine. She'd taken her heels off when they entered the hotel room. And the carpet felt plush and soft under her feet. She walked toward the plate glass windows, which offered a view of the city skyline. Mads had texted Jessie to make sure that Sofia was okay and Iona walked over to look out at the city. Snow had fallen earlier and she could see the white blanket on the grassy areas below. She put her forehead on the glass and took a minute to enjoy how peaceful Manhattan looked tonight.

She heard Mads behind her before she felt the heat from his

body and his hand on the back of her neck. He ran his finger along the top strand of pearls on her choker. His finger was warm and his touch light, but a shiver went down her spine at his touch. It had been too long since she'd been in his arms.

She knew that it had been her decision, but she'd missed him.

She had wanted to be sure that this wasn't just a Christmas fling. Her instant reaction to being alone, but the last few weeks had convinced her that what she felt for Mads was real and tonight, meeting his friends and work colleagues, had demonstrated to her that she meant something to him too. More than one of the spouses of the board members had remarked to her how happy Mads seemed.

She was so glad to see that he was coming out of his grief. Moving forward. With her.

She turned her head to look at him and he arched one eyebrow at her as he drew his forefinger down her back towards the band at the top of her dress. He ran his fingertip along the edge where fabric and skin met. Another shiver went through her as he slowly moved his touch towards her side where the zipper was nestled under her arm. She lifted her arm slightly to allow him access, but instead of lowering it he simply ran his finger over it, brushing the side of her breast, which made the tip tighten and then he put his open palm on her butt, caressing the full curve before slowly bringing his touch up the other side of her body.

Shivering with longing and need she tried to turn to face him, but he put one hand on the small of her back, keeping her facing away from him.

She felt the warm exhalation of his breath before she felt the brush of his lips at the base of her neck, just under the bottom strand of pearls. One of his arms came around her waist and he drew her back against his body. She put her hand over his wrist to hold on to him. Realizing she still wore her gloves, she reached up to take it off and he helped her. Then he lowered the zipper at the side of her dress and stepped back.

The velvet dress had stays in the bodice and she delicately stepped out of it, standing in front of him wearing just her panties and pearls.

His pupils were dilated and she saw the flush of arousal on his skin. He reached out to touch her, drawing his hand slowly over the curves of her body, before lifting her up in his arms and carrying her to the bed. He set her down on it, undoing his pants and freeing his erection. She shifted around, pushing her panties down her legs and kicking them off and then opening her arms to beckon him to her.

Taking her hips in his hands, he drew her forward until her backside was on the edge of the bed and then he leaned over her, brushing his shirt front over her aroused nipples as his mouth found hers. She felt him between her legs, just the tip of him and then he pushed in deeper and she opened her eyes and saw he was watching her and she felt her heart skip a beat. The combination of desire, tenderness, and affection made her realize that she'd found the home she'd been searching for in Mads. He thrust deeper into her and passion drove out all her thoughts.

She held on to him as if she'd never let him go. She wrapped her legs around his waist as he thrust faster and deeper into her, arching off the bed as she called his name, holding onto him as he continued to thrust inside of her until he collapsed, rolling to his side and holding her to him.

She ran her fingers over his chest, trying to catch her breath, lifted her head to look at him, but he kissed her again, shifting them both on the bed until she was cuddled close to his side.

"This has been the best night of my life," she whispered, kissing the pad of his chest over his heart.

"Mine too," he admitted, running his hand through her hair and pulling the pins from it until the long strands fell on her shoulders and he drew a few of the strands over her shoulder.

She looked up at him and caught a glimpse of sadness in his eyes, worried that he might be remembering his past, but then he made love to her again, more tenderly this time, and she fell into an exhausted sleep dreaming of herself and Mads and Sofia walking in a winter wonderland.

Chapter 20

It was the Friday before Christmas and Iona hadn't heard from Mads since the party at the Common two days earlier. He'd made love to her and then the next morning she'd woke up alone in the Presidential Suite. He'd left a note on the nightstand saying he had an early meeting and he'd be in touch soon.

But every time she texted him she got back a smiley face or a message saying he was busy. Sofia was staying at the Common visiting her maternal grandparents who'd come out from the West Coast to see her for a few days, but Iona knew she was meant to be back later on this evening and she was tired of waiting to hear from Mads. So she'd been reduced to waiting by her own front door, listening for the sound of footfalls in the hallway.

She heard the elevator ping and opened the door just as Mads stepped out of the car. He saw her and she suspected he'd wanted to turn and go back downstairs. Mainly because she saw the way he half-turned.

"Mads. We need to talk," she said.

He glanced at his watch.

"I don't care how busy you are. I think you can give me five minutes of your time."

He rubbed the back of his neck. A gesture she knew he did

when he was feeling a little bit stressed and she steeled herself from feeling sorry for him. He was avoiding her. He'd made love to her like she was the woman he wanted to spend the rest of his life with and then he'd ghosted out of her life. And she'd done it herself a time or two, so she knew what he was doing.

"Iona, please could this wait? I have to go and get Sofia and her grandparents and take them to the airport."

"I know that. Which is why I thought it would have been nice to speak earlier this week, but you have been avoiding me."

"Let's get out of the hall so we can talk," he said.

There was a flatness to his voice that she'd never heard before and she had the feeling that whatever it was she'd thought the other night meant it hadn't meant the same thing to him at all.

She stepped back into her apartment and he followed her in. She heard him close the door, but she kept walking down the hall to her living room. She propped her hip on the edge of the love seat as Mads followed her into the room. He still had his coat on and she noticed there were snowflakes on his shoulders. But the thought of a white Christmas didn't lift her spirits.

"What is going on?" she asked. "I thought we had a really great time the other night."

"We did have a nice time," he said flatly. "But that's all it was."

"Stop. I'm not going to buy that."

"What do you want from me?" he asked.

"Just tell me *what's* going on."

Mads looked down at the floor and then looked back up at her. "I can't love you the way you want to be loved, Iona. There is a part of me that always thought that one day I'd meet another woman and I'd be able to settle into a marriage and life with her as much for companionship for myself and a mother figure for Sofia. But meeting you has shown me how wrong I was."

Iona felt a weight like a stone in the pit of her stomach. "What do you mean? I love Sofia and you and I get along really well together."

"We do. But it won't last. I can't let myself fall for you, Iona. There is a part of me that is afraid that as soon as I do something will happen to you. And that's not fair to you or to Sofia. She already loves you and I don't want to see her hurt when you realize I can't love you."

"What?" she said again. Not comprehending how he could think that she'd ever abandoned his daughter. It was easier to focus on that than the fact that he said he couldn't love her. She didn't want to allow herself to let those words sink in, they made him seem icier than she'd thought he was.

Had she simply seen something she had wanted to see instead of the truth? "I would *never* hurt Sofia. Already I love her like she was a daughter to me. She's sweet and funny and she wants so badly to see some sign of the magic in the world around her. She is starting to see it in Christmas but she'd never want to disappoint you."

"And I don't want to disappoint her," Mads said. "I know you wouldn't want to hurt her …"

"Stop. It sounds to me like you are using Sofia as the reason why we can't be together. I'm not going to hurt her. Even if you walk out of here and say you never want to see me again, I'll always be a friend to your daughter."

***

He knew that Iona would be there for Sofia. That was the kind of woman she was, which made this so much harder. He had never felt anything like this for another person, not even Gill, and that scared him more than spending the rest of his life alone. No matter how bad he felt at this moment, it was better to have a clean break and walk away now.

"It's not an excuse," he said, then knew he was going to have to make it clear he was ending things. Iona was still arguing with him like she could change his mind. And maybe she could change his mind, but his heart had already decided it couldn't take the risk of loving her. "You forget that we'd never intended to start dating. We kind of drifted together. And I'll always be grateful for it, but this is it."

Her eyes widened and color swept up her neck and she crossed her arms over her chest. "What is wrong with you? We slept together. And you might want to pretend now that it meant nothing to you but I remember the first time, when you cried. When I held you and we both were more vulnerable than we'd ever allowed ourselves to be before that."

He cursed. He saw the shock on her face as she stepped back from him. "I can't do this, Iona. I'm not going to risk falling in love with you and starting to plan a life, only to have it ripped away from me. And I'm not like you, I don't believe in Santa or any of the other fairy tales you like to spout. Real life hurts and it's not fair and it can take someone who has nothing left to lose and show him something so perfect and good just to rip it away from him. I can't do it.

"Mads, I can. I'm willing to take the risk," she said.

"I'm not. This is it. This is goodbye. There isn't anything you can say that will convince me otherwise."

"You're a coward," she said. "I never thought that I'd say that to you because I've seen you with your daughter and I know what you've been through. But I can't help it."

"Fine. Call me names if it makes you feel better. You've never watched someone you love slip away slowly over the course of three years. You haven't prayed and begged God for a miracle or comforted your child because she won't know her mother growing up. I've been strong for longer than anyone ever should be expected to be."

He stalked over to her. Looked down into her eyes and saw them filling with tears. And knew that this was something he wouldn't want to remember, but suspected that her face would haunt him for the rest of his life.

"But I did it. And I promised myself never again. I didn't think it was possible that I could care for anyone again. So that part was easy at first. But meeting you was unexpected. It jarred me."

"That's what you needed," she said, through her tears. "I know you think that this is one-sided, but it's not. We both were broken. I think we have something special here."

"Maybe it was what I needed. But I can't let myself give in to my emotions again. It's hard enough worrying about Sofia. I can't even let her fly anywhere."

"Fine. I'll take whatever you can give me," she said, crossing the room and reaching for him. "I love you, Mads."

His heart took a punch. He hadn't been expecting that. He stepped back from her, knowing that if she touched him he'd give in now only to hurt her later. "I can't do that to you. You have told me about the men in your past. How you've always been the one to fix them so they can find love and I want to do that for you. I want to be the man who makes it so you can find your happy ending."

"I don't think it works that way," she said.

"I have to believe it can," he said. "Because I want you to find a man who can love you the way you deserve to be loved."

She shook her head. There was an aura around her that he'd never seen before and he wondered what was going through her head. He was doing this for her. For both of them. He admitted he couldn't risk losing her. Risk loving her and then losing her. He wasn't doing that again.

"The heart doesn't work that way," she said quietly.

"In time it will feel different," he said. "Good bye, Iona."

He forced himself to turn and walk to the door because he knew he had to leave. And there was a part of him that wanted her to convince him to stay. A part of him that wanted to believe her when she said that whatever he could give would be enough. He knew that wasn't true. It wouldn't be good enough for him and he'd hate himself for ruining her feisty spirit and innocent belief in the world.

He opened the door to the hallway, aware that she'd stayed in the living room and let himself out of her apartment. He walked further down to his own apartment and let himself inside. It was empty and quiet since Jessie was on vacation until January and Sofia was at the Common with her grandparents. Mads took no comfort from it. He'd done what he had to do in order to protect her and some day he might be able to feel good about it, but right now he just felt hollow and empty inside.

***

Iona took the pint of Minty Wonderland ice cream out of the freezer and went back into her living room. Last night she'd been okay, but this morning the break-up hit her hard. She'd made a run to the nearest bodega and loaded up on junk food. So far, she'd decimated two packages of Little Debbie Christmas Tree Cakes and had been watching *It's A Wonderful Life* on repeat, since that was the one movie that made her cry like nothing else. And she was crying anyway.

Her mom was at one of her charities and Iona had refused to call her away from that. But she really could use her mom. So she'd texted her to stop by if she had a minute and that had led to a phone call, more crying and her mom's promise she'd be by later today.

Her front door opened after a perfunctory knock.

"Io?" Cici called. "You're mom called us. We came as soon as we could."

"Where are you?" Hayley called out.

She heard the jingle of Lucy's collar and the cooing of baby Holly as her friends came into the living room. Iona tried to sit up on the couch but she had piled the pillows behind her back and it was awkward. The ice cream slipped from her hand onto her lap.

"You're a mess," Hayley said, scooping up the ice cream and putting it on the coffee table before pulling her into a tight bear hug.

"Why are you watching this sob fest?" Cici asked, putting baby Holly's carrier on the floor before coming over to hug her too.

"I was crying anyway," she said.

"Are you cried-out?"

She shook her head.

That just made her cry a little bit more. She didn't understand his reasons for breaking up with her but she knew they were valid in his eyes. Cici located the remote and turned off the television, just as an angel was getting his wings.

Lucy hopped up on the couch and climbed on to Iona's lap and she petted the little dog, admitting to herself that she was happy to see her friends.

Hayley took the ice cream to the kitchen and Cici cleaned up the wrappers that littered the floor around her. She was embarrassed by how messy she'd been. Then Cici took Holly from her carrier and sat down on the coach next to Iona.

"What happened?"

"I don't know. I mean we had a fight, but I don't understand where it came from," Iona said.

"Tell us about it," Hayley said. "We'll help you figure it out."

"All right, things have been off between us since Tuesday night when we went to the party at the Common. The entire night felt so special and magical. I knew then that I love Mads and there was something about him that made me think he loved me too. But then he didn't call or answer my texts and so last night I sat by the front door waiting for him to come home."

"Oh, Iona … what happened?

Iona tucked a strand of hair back behind her ear and realized how greasy it felt. Sure, it had only been one day since she'd showered but her entire body seemed to be getting into it.

"I don't know. He said that he thought maybe our relationship was for him to show me there was more to life than just work. So I could go on to love someone else," she said as her voice cracked a little bit. "He can't love me the way I deserve."

"That's crazy," Hayley said. "Completely bonkers, but a very nice sentiment."

"I think he's just afraid to get hurt again," Cici said. "And he doesn't want you to get hurt either."

"Are you guys on my side or not?" Iona asked. She'd already figured all of that out last night at about two a.m., when she'd been sleeping in the guest bedroom because she'd had sex with Mads on the couch and in her bed so she hadn't been able to sleep in either of those places.

"We're on your side," Cici said, as Holly got fussy and Cici undid her blouse to breastfeed.

"You know what I think you should do? Just keep on seeing him like you have been," Hayley said. "Just as friends. That should make him crack. We already know he cares for you."

"I wonder if he's lost the ability to really care or maybe it's too soon. Blair said that he was complicated and I should have listened to her," Iona said.

Cici sighed. "I don't know if you will be able to change his mind. What about Sofia?"

"I don't know. Of course, I'm still her friend but I don't know if Mads will discourage her from seeing me," Iona said.

"Time will tell," Hayley said. "But for now, let's get you out of this funk."

She didn't want to have to get through anything. She had finally opened her heart to love and somehow she'd thought that would be enough, but of course it wasn't. But with her friends in her apartment she no longer felt like turning into a hermit and eating until none of her clothes fit her.

Hayley and Cici stayed until lunchtime, making sure that Iona got showered and dressed and went with her to the retirement home, where she was supposed to sing carols and distribute

199

cookies. She appreciated her friends and knew getting out of the apartment would help her but she couldn't help remembering that Mads and Sofia were supposed to be with her. She had tucked her gifts for both of them in her bag and decided she'd ask the doorman to give them to them both when she returned.

Chapter 21

Sofia wasn't too happy when he told her that they weren't going to be going with Iona to sing carols. But Mads had made up his mind. It would be easier for both of them if they just got used to not having her around.

When there was a knock on the door Sofia jumped off the couch and ran for the door. He suspected she was hoping it would be Iona, but he knew she wouldn't just show up. That wasn't her way.

Instead it was the doorman, Greg.

"Hello, Greg."

"Hi, Sofia. These presents were left downstairs for you. I figured you'd want them, so I brought them up."

Mads, who had followed Sofia to the door, reached around her to take the gaily wrapped packages. "Thank you."

He saw the disappointment on Sofia's face as she glanced around him down the hallway, no doubt looking for Iona.

Greg gave her a smile and then turned to leave and Mads closed the door behind him.

They went back into the living room and Mads looked at the packages, realizing he recognized Iona's handwriting on them.

"Do you want to open your present now?" he asked.

"But it's not Christmas. I thought we had to wait," she said.

"I think we could both use some cheering up. And this is our year to do things differently," he said. Reminding himself that he was supposed to be making this Christmas different, not still feeling so broken and alone.

"Yay. Yes, I want to open it," she said.

She came over to the large armchair where he usually sat in the living room and climbed up on his lap. The presents were large and there was one for each of them. Sofia took hers. "I have something for Iona too."

"I know you do. We will ask Greg to deliver it to her."

"Okay. Or maybe I could go down there," she said.

Mads didn't want to isolate his daughter from Iona, so he nodded. "Maybe. Why don't we see what she got for you?"

Sofia nodded and then tore at the paper the way she always did. She handed him the parts she ripped off and he balled them up, setting them on the side table next to his chair.

The box was plain white and she carefully opened it up. Inside was a paperback of *A Visit from St. Nicholas*. And when Sofia opened it up, Mads saw that Iona had doctored the book the way that Gill had done for Sofia's knight book. Mads' picture had been used for Santa and the sleeping children were Sofia and Holly and the reindeer were all Lucy, the little miniature dachshund. And then at the end of the story was the picture that they had posed for at the *Nutcracker* and underneath it Iona had written: *Santa can deliver special presents, but only love can make a family. Merry Christmas.*

"Oh, Papa, I love it," Sofia said. Then underneath the book was a Christmas ornament of a knight wearing a dress just like in the book that Gill had made for Sofia.

Mads hugged his daughter close, knowing that he couldn't let Iona go. She was the missing part of their family. Just like they were hers. And it didn't matter if he tried to protect himself by never seeing her again, he was going to love her for the rest of his life.

Sofia hopped off his lap and walked over to the tree, putting the ornament next to the angel that he and Gill had given her last year for Christmas. "Look, Papa, it's me and Mommy."

"It is the both of you," Mads said.

"What did Iona give you?" Sofia asked. "I love my present, Papa."

"I know, sweetheart, it's perfect."

"It is. I just got her a scarf. I think I better do something else," Sofia said.

Mads opened his present and saw that it was a photo book. Sofia climbed up on his lap. The front cover said Eriksson Traditions. And when he opened it he saw photos of him and Sofia from this Christmas season. In their ugly sweaters, eating gingerbread at the Common, ice skating with Remy's family, decorating their tree, baking cookies. She'd written another note, this one slipped inside on a piece of paper.

I know that you and Sofia will continue to find the traditions that define your family and at the heart of them will be the love you share.

Sofia curled up in his arms and he held his daughter, knowing that he had made a mistake when he'd told Iona that he couldn't love her. These gifts were unconditional and maybe he might end up being a very overprotective husband, but he knew he was going to ask Iona to share the rest of her life with him and Sofia.

But he had to figure out how to do it. He was going to need a big gesture to show her what was in his heart. And to convince her that he loved her, the way she deserved to be loved.

"Sofia, I need your help," he said, when the idea came to him. "With what?"

"Making some Christmas magic for Iona," Mads said. "Show her how much she means to both of us."

"I'm in," she said, with her gap-toothed grin. Together they worked hard on their plan and he had to recruit some outside help with her friends and they were much nicer this time when he texted them than they had been the last time.

Now all he had to do was hope that he hadn't killed the love she had for him. That she would be willing to take a chance on him.

***

Mads was sweating inside the suit he wore. He wasn't sure that Hayley and Cici would be able to convince Iona to join them for dinner in the Common's private dining room. But they both were certain it would happen. His brother was keeping watch at the door that led from the food and beverage hallway into the room. Sofia looked adorable in her Santa's helper outfit. She had on a pair of striped red and white tights and a red velvet dress trimmed in white faux fur, with a Santa hat on her head that jingled when she moved. And she kept moving around. She'd wanted to wear shoes with bells on them too but they hadn't been able to find any on such short notice.

"She's here," Piers said. "And it looks like they invited about twenty people to dinner."

"Are you kidding me?"

"Nope. I guess they wanted some witnesses to this," Piers said.

"Great," Mads said.

"It is great, Papa," Sofia said.

Well, it would be great if things went well. If they didn't then … well then, he'd just deal with it. He wasn't going to change his mind if there were five people in the other room or one hundred. He loved Iona and he'd hurt her; he wanted to make her happy and needed to convince her that he was sincere.

Sofia squeezed between him and Piers, poking her head through the opening to see into the room. They were all sitting down at the long table that had been set up for them.

"Are you ready?" Piers asked.

"As I'll ever be," Mads said.

"Sof?"

"I am," she said, smiling up at them both.

The music switched from *Greensleeves* to *Santa Claus is Coming to Town*. And Sofia skipped into the room, bells jingling as she danced to the head of the table where Iona was seated.

Mads stood in the doorway watching Iona's face as his daughter stopped right next to her.

"Hello. I'm Santa's helper and he's here to bring presents to all the good boys and girls."

"Hello there. I thought you didn't believe in Santa," Iona said, unable to hide her surprise.

"A good friend told me that Santa takes care of special gifts. I think that you deserve one."

"Is Santa bringing it to me?" she asked.

"He is," Sofia confirmed.

Mads walked into the room in his red Santa suit, wearing a Santa hat, and stopped when he was a few feet from Iona. She had her chair turned to the side so they were facing each other.

"Santa?"

"Yup. That's him," Sofia said.

Suddenly all the words he'd rehearsed and the clever lines he'd practiced just disappeared and all he could think about was Iona. He closed the gap between them. "I wanted to tell you how you brought the magic of Christmas back into my life. How you showed me that love was strong enough to overcome fear, but the truth is I'm still scared. The only difference is that now I'm afraid of what my life will be like if I can't convince you to take a chance on me ..."

"Us," Sofia added. "Both of us."

Mads looked at his daughter and then reached out for her, she took his hand and they turned to Iona. "I was wrong when I said I couldn't be the man for you. That maybe I was trying to heal you for someone else. That's impossible because no one could love you more than I do. I thought you'd be safer and happier without me by your side, but that's not true."

"No it's not," Iona said, getting to her feet and coming over to him.

He leaned in until their foreheads touched and then he whispered, "I love you."

"Are you sure?" she whispered back.

"Yes, I am," he said, their eyes met and he hoped she could see how much he loved and needed her.

She wrapped her arms around his shoulders and he lifted her off her feet as he kissed her.

Their friends and family all cheered and he set her on her feet, reaching for the red velvet bag that Sofia held. "I know we haven't known each other that long, but I want you to know that one day I intend to make you my wife. Until then I hope you will wear this ring."

He took the box from the bag and handed it to her. Inside was a simple band made up of hearts that Sofia had helped him pick out. Iona nodded and put the ring on her finger. "I can't wait for that day."

Mads, Piers, and Sofia joined the group for Christmas Eve dinner and when they went home that night and Mads took Iona in his arms and made love to her, he knew he'd found a Christmas gift he hadn't expected. He'd been lucky to have found love once in his life but twice made him believe in miracles and all sorts of things that he never had before.

Epilogue

Christmas was the most special time of the year. This year, Iona Eriksson knew that no matter how much she loved decorating the Candied Apple Café and designing the windows, coming home to the brownstone that she shared with her family was when she felt the real magic of Christmas.

She opened the door and heard the sound of Sofia singing *Must Be Santa* along with Bob Dylan. Iona hurried down the hall and stood in the doorway watching Sofia dancing around Mads, who was cuddling their three-month-old son, Alexander, in his arms. The baby was cooing as Sofia and Mads sang and danced around the Christmas tree that was partially decorated.

Iona joined in signing and Sofia turned to her. "Mama, you're home early."

She ran to Iona, who leaned down to scoop her up. She joined the men to dance and sing, her eyes met Mads and she felt a fullness in her heart that she had never known she'd find. Her father had been a man who's shown her success came from dividing her personal and business lives, but Iona had found true happiness and success by blending the two.

She'd been touched when Sofia had asked to call her "mama", telling Iona that her mommy was in heaven but she wanted to have the same mama as Alexander.

"Tonight's the night we go to visit Santa," Iona said. Both she and Mads had been surprised when Sofia had expressed an interest in visiting him at the big Macy's department store, but it had made them happy to hear it. So much had changed in the last year for all of them. Mads and she were still finding their footing together as a couple, but after being married in a small family-only ceremony back in February after Iona had realized she was pregnant, both of them had known they wanted to spend their life together. Though Iona had thought they'd have a little bit longer to get used to being a family.

It turned out that they hadn't needed the time.

The doorbell rang and Sofia squirmed to get out of Iona's arms, racing for the front door. Cici, Hoop, and Holly were there. Cici looked a little pale, but that was to be expected as she had just announced she was expecting.

Iona couldn't be more thrilled for her friend. Hayley so far was resisting the lure of motherhood due to her crazy early morning schedule at the Candied Apple Café but Garrett had taken another promotion at work, which meant a regular schedule as opposed to his days as a beat cop, so Iona suspected they'd be parents soon.

Even Theo and Nico were parents to Kasim and Leo, twin boys who they were fostering but hoped to adopt in the coming year. As her friends came in and the kids laughed and talked, Iona couldn't help but feel like she'd been given the best gift of all when Mads had surprised her at the Candied Apple Café last year.

He came up behind her, wrapping her in one arm as she took her son from him and looked down into those blue eyes that reminded her of Mads.

"Happy?"

"More than I could have ever believed. You?"

"Yes. I've been so blessed to know the love of two women and to be able to share my life with you."

Read on for Naughty & Nice Truffle recipes inspired by *Christmas at the Candied Apple Café*, by Katherine Garbera

Naughty Truffle (spicy dark chocolate truffle)

Ingredients
2/3 cup heavy cream
1/4 teaspoon ground cinnamon
1/4 teaspoon chili powder
1/8 teaspoon cayenne pepper
12 ounces dark chocolate, chopped
1/3 cup of red colored sugar

Directions
In a medium saucepot, heat the cream, cinnamon, chili powder and cayenne pepper over medium-low heat until it comes to a simmer. Add the chocolate and stir until the chocolate is completely melted. Transfer to a bowl and chill in the refrigerator until it firms up, 1 1/2 to 2 hours.

Place the red colored sugar onto a small plate.

Remove the chocolate from the refrigerator and let sit for 30 minutes to soften.
Using a small ice cream scoop or tablespoon, scoop out the chocolate into the red colored sugar and roll them around to completely coat. Place on a plate and serve. Truffles can be stored in the refrigerator for 2 days in an airtight container.

Nice Truffle (Sweet white chocolate truffle)

Ingredients
2 tablespoons heavy cream

7 ounces of chopped white chocolate
2 tablespoons vanilla extract
6 ounces chopped dark chocolate
1/3 cup green colored sugar

Directions

Place the cream in a heat-proof bowl, and set the bowl over a pan of simmering water. Cook until heated through. Using a wire whisk, slowly stir the white chocolate into the warm cream until completely melted. Whisk in the vanilla. Cover and chill for 1 hour or until pliable but firm enough to scoop.

With 2 teaspoons or a 1 1/4-inch ice cream scoop, make dollops of the chocolate mixture and place on a baking sheet lined with parchment paper. Refrigerate for about 15 minutes, until firm enough to roll into rough spheres. Melt the dark chocolate in a heat-proof bowl, set over a pan of simmering water. Drizzle the melted dark chocolate over 10 of the truffles. Roll the remaining truffles in the green colored sugar. Chill until ready to serve.

Acknowledgements

I have to thank Charlotte Ledger my wonderful editor for her patience and support when I said I wanted to write a book where the heroine had slept with a guy, got pregnant and he wasn't the hero. Also, thanks to Eve and Nancy who spent endless hours on FaceTime with me as I wrote this book and needed a sounding block. As always, every book I write is made possible by the support of my loving husband Rob Elser and my two kiddos Courtney & Lucas.

Printed by RR Donnelley at Glasgow, UK